THE RIGID DUKE

DARCY BURKE

ZEALOUS QUILL PRESS

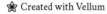

THE RIGID DUKE

**The course of true love never runs smooth.
Sometimes a little matchmaking is required.**

As a refinement tutor, Mrs. Juno Langton helps young ladies develop the skills and confidence to secure an advantageous marriage. Her cheerful disposition never wavers no matter how challenging her assignment. When a house party provides an opportunity to match her difficult charge with a duke, Juno will go to any lengths to satisfy her employer and ensure the young lady's future. Too bad the duke is an unsmiling, rigid grouch, albeit an irritatingly handsome one.

The Duke of Warrington dislikes social gatherings and despises the Marriage Mart which makes it nigh impossible to find a wife. He plans to secure his future duchess at a house party, but she's being managed by a thoroughly meddlesome—and provocative—Mrs. Langton, who is determined to find his better nature. He'll do anything to avoid her sunny charm and room-brightening smiles, but she's breaking through his shell and the only way he can think to keep her quiet is to kiss her. He must marry the young lady, not desire the companion.

But now he's rethinking his wife choices.

Don't miss the rest of the *Matchmaking Chronicles*!

Do you want to hear all the latest about me and my books? Sign up at Reader Club newsletter for members-only bonus content, advance notice of pre-orders, insider scoop, as well as contests and giveaways!

Care to share your love for my books with like-minded readers? Want to hang with me and see pictures of my cats (who doesn't!)? Then don't miss my exclusive Facebook groups!

Darcy's Duchesses for historical readers
Burke's Book Lovers for contemporary readers

CHAPTER 1

"*M*arina has made a great deal of progress this summer." Mrs. Juno Langton smiled brightly at her employer, Lady Wetherby. "I daresay she could attempt a short stint in York this fall."

With a wide, furrowed brow and pursed lips, Lady Wetherby didn't appear convinced. But why should she? Her daughter, Marina, was a social disaster. *Was.* Juno's job was to fix that, and she *had* made some progress. However, perhaps describing it as "a great deal" was a slight exaggeration.

"In what specific ways has she improved?" the countess asked from the opposite chair in her private sitting room, where they met weekly to discuss Marina.

"Her dancing." Because they practiced over an hour every day. "Her ease at conversation." Also because they practiced over an hour every day. And Juno wasn't shortsighted about it—she knew Marina's comfort had increased with *her*, but would take some finessing once they got to London. Or York, which would be an excellent rehearsal for London.

"What about smiling?" Lady Wetherby asked. "I

haven't seen her smile any more than she did before. Which was hardly at all." She gave her head a tiny shake.

"That is also improving." Again, Juno had found success with Marina, but couldn't be certain her charge would smile with other people. At least not at first. That was the problem. Until Marina got to know someone, she was completely uncomfortable in their presence. She didn't make eye contact, she fidgeted, and she barely said a word. Juno could well imagine how it was that no gentleman danced with her a second time—not at a single ball but during the *entire* Season.

"I'm not seeing it, but then I think Marina takes pleasure in behaving in an especially surly manner with me." Lady Wetherby's lips pursed even more. Juno wondered if they might shrivel up and disappear.

"I don't believe that's true, my lady," Juno said with a reassuring smile. "I think, with respect, that Marina wants to please you and knows she hasn't."

Lady Wetherby's nostrils flared. "Are you saying it's my fault she's cold and awkward?"

"Not at all." Though she wasn't terribly wrong… "Perhaps if you gave her more encouragement, you might be rewarded with her demonstrating the progress she's made." Juno offered her widest smile, which typically thawed even the most frigid people. Not that Lady Wetherby was frigid. Well, perhaps she was when it came to her eldest child. Juno had seen the countess with her younger children, and she seemed far more relaxed.

"I'll do that," Lady Wetherby said before exhaling a rather beleaguered sigh. "I'm sure you're right that she is making progress. That is the reason we hired you after departing London early."

Juno had finished her prior contract of employment sooner than she'd planned when her former charge had snared an earl. The family had been overjoyed with Juno's tutelage, and Juno had been thrilled to take some time for herself, adjourning to Bath, where she'd spent a lovely fortnight in the strong arms of a charming captain. It might have been longer except she'd received the offer from the Wetherbys to attend their daughter, who was in dire need of refinement after a disastrous first Season. Unable to resist the challenge—or the pay —Juno had left her captain and traveled north to Yorkshire.

"I do fear she is destined for spinsterhood," Lady Wetherby said with a frown, drawing Juno back to the present.

"I am confident we can avoid that. The right husband is out there for Marina. We just have to find him. I do think a short stint to York may be just the thing." Juno wanted Marina to be able to practice her newfound skills in social settings outside the bustle and pressure of the Season.

"I agree," Lady Wetherby said, clasping her hands in her lap. "Not about York, but that the right husband is out there. To that end, we've been invited to a house party next month. The Duke of Warrington will be in attendance. He is rumored to detest the Marriage Mart, but is also in need of a wife. It's the perfect opportunity to secure a match between him and Marina." Her blue eyes positively glowed with anticipation and confidence. As if the betrothal between Marina and the duke were a *fait accompli.*

Juno was only vaguely aware of the duke. He did not seem to be a social sort, which made it easy to believe that he didn't care for the Marriage Mart. Matching someone like him with someone like Marina would be...challenging.

Juno absolutely loved a challenge. That was how she'd embarked on this career of helping young ladies bring their natural confidence and charm to the fore following the death of her husband. Dashing Bernard Langton had swept a naïve young Juno into a mad love affair and marriage, shocking her parents and prompting them to disassociate from their only daughter.

After less than a year, Bernard had died, leaving Juno without family or funds. She'd leapt at the chance to be companion to an elderly lady. When she'd helped that lady's granddaughter secure an upwardly mobile marriage, Juno's career as a companion, or more accurately "refinement tutor," had been born.

"Shall I summon Marina to join us?" Juno suggested, hoping her charge would be up to the task of gaining her mother's approval. That was, unfortunately, no small feat.

"I asked Dale to send her in after a while." Lady Wetherby directed her gaze to the doorway, which was behind Juno. "Here she is."

Juno turned her head to see Marina walk cautiously into the sitting room. Dressed in a simple pale blue day gown, Marina fidgeted with her fingers as she approached, her blue eyes downcast.

"Look up, dear," Lady Wetherby said with a bit of snap to her tone.

"Come and join us, Marina." Juno stood and moved to a settee so Marina could sit beside her.

Marina's gaze lifted to briefly meet Juno's before she moved to the settee. Once seated, she plucked at the skirt of her gown.

"Do stop that." Lady Wetherby frowned at her daughter.

Juno edged closer to Marina, hoping her presence would be a comforting influence. "We have exciting news to share."

Marina glanced toward her as her fingers stilled. Straightening, she sat as Juno had taught her—shoulders back, spine stiff, chin up, slight smile in place. Pride shot through Juno, as well as glee that Marina had found the courage to do what she must in her mother's presence.

Lady Wetherby's features flashed with surprise and perhaps a dash of approval. "We are to attend a house party next month. The Duke of Warrington will be in attendance, and he is in search of a wife. My darling, you could snag a duke without having to suffer another Season."

Juno felt a burst of tenderness at the warmth in the countess's tone. She might be frustrated by her daughter—and certainly didn't understand her—but she wanted the best for her, including the chance to avoid a Season, which she knew Marina had loathed.

Instead of responding with relief at this prospect, Marina crumpled, her face falling into a deep scowl. "Must I, Mother?"

"I'm afraid so." The countess had stiffened, her face freezing in disappointment. "I do hope you can summon the appropriate enthusiasm."

Turning toward her charge, Juno gently touched the young woman's arm. "Just think, you'll have a chance to practice everything we've worked on. A house party is the perfect place to gain confidence and hone your skills."

"I barely have any of either," Marina said quietly, shooting a perturbed look toward her mother. "But I suppose I have no choice."

"That is correct," Lady Wetherby said firmly. "We leave in a fortnight." Her expression gentled once more. "The duke doesn't care for the Marriage Mart either. Perhaps the two of you will find an accord. I think this could be just the match you've been waiting for."

"I haven't been waiting for any match," Marina muttered. "May I go now?"

"Yes." The countess looked rather despondent as her daughter stood and shuffled from the room.

Juno tensed as she readjusted herself on the settee to face her employer. "She'll be ready for the house party. She just needs to acclimate herself. We've plenty of time to prepare."

"I hope you're right, considering what I'm paying you. In fact, if you can ensure this betrothal occurs, I'll increase your pay twenty percent." Lady Wetherby stood. "Do not let us down, Mrs. Langton."

The countess swept from the room, and Juno narrowed her eyes in contemplation. A fortnight to not only ensure Marina was ready for a house party, but that she could snare a duke. It would be Juno's most daunting challenge yet.

She leapt to her feet, eager to get started.

~

*A*lexander Brett, Duke of Warrington, stalked into the drawing room at precisely a quarter of an hour before six. His mother, seated serenely on the dark red settee, came from the dower house most evenings to dine with him.

She surveyed him as he went to pour a glass of her favorite madeira and a brandy for himself. "How was your day?"

After handing her the wine, he sat in the chair near her settee. Same drinks, same seating arrangement, same question to begin their conversation. He liked same.

"Productive."

"As always," she murmured. "I don't suppose anything exciting happened?"

"The post was greater than usual." He sipped his brandy.

"Anything of interest?"

"Not to me, though you would probably find the invitation to a house party notable."

His mother, in her early fifties with still-dark hair, save a few strands of gray at her temples, sat a bit taller. "What house party? When?" Her sable eyes sparked with enthusiasm.

"Doesn't matter. I'm not going."

She pursed her lips at him before relaxing. He could see she was choosing her words, lining up her soldiers for the coming battle. "But you should. I realize you don't care for social situations; however, this is a small gathering, not at all like the events of the Season."

Dare, the name he'd been called his entire life, which was a shortened version of the courtesy title he'd held—Marquess of Daresbury—before his father's death three years earlier, narrowed his eyes at his mother. "You're behind this invitation."

"What makes you think that?" She tried to sound innocent, but her gaze darted to the side and her voice rose. When he said nothing, she looked back to him and exhaled. "Fine. Yes."

"Am I to understand you convinced Lady Cosford to host a house party so that I might attend?"

"Of course not. I merely made a few well-placed comments to friends in recent months."

"What sort of comments?"

"That you are in search of a wife." She gave him an exasperated look. "Well, you *are*." Frowning at him, she took an irritated sip of madeira.

"And that somehow led to an invitation to a

house party that I have no desire to attend." He made a sound low in his throat before taking another drink of brandy.

"Don't growl. It's so off-putting."

"I don't growl."

His mother arched a thick, dark brow, then shook her head, apparently deciding that was a battle she didn't care to wage. "You should accept the invitation. You do need a wife, and I should think finding one at a small house party in Warwickshire would be far more appealing than attempting the Marriage Mart in London come spring."

Dare shuddered. He couldn't think of anything he'd rather do less. His mother was, unfortunately, correct. He did need a wife. Furthermore, he'd been lamenting how he might find one given that he hated, as his mother had put it, social situations.

What if there wasn't anyone at the house party he would consider marrying? He scrutinized his mother and gave her the credit she was due. "What is the young lady's name?"

She looked at him in surprise, as if he couldn't guess she was scheming a particular match. Faint pink brightened her cheeks, but the color was fleeting. "Lady Marina Fellowes, eldest daughter of the Earl of Wetherby. I'm sure you know him."

They worked together in the House of Lords. Wetherby didn't care for idle chatter and always got right to the heart of things. Dare hadn't even realized he had a daughter. Or a family, for that matter. Perhaps his daughter wouldn't be the typical prattle basket that most young ladies were.

"What's she like?" he asked cautiously.

The vigor with which his mother answered almost made him sorry he'd expressed even the slightest interest. "Very pretty and quite accomplished at needlework."

"That tells me nothing. Is she a featherbrain or not?"

"I doubt it."

That was not a promising answer. Perhaps his mother didn't know her. "Has she even had a Season?"

"Yes, just this past one." His mother's features brightened. "You should like this bit. She returned to the country early. I'm not sure London—rather, the social whirl—is to her liking."

"You should have started with that," Dare muttered. If Lady Marina was cut from the same cloth as her father—and why wouldn't she be?—this house party actually had potential. "I'll go to the party to meet Lady Marina."

"To see if you will suit?"

Dare glowered at his mother's obvious glee. "Yes."

She laughed. "You always try so hard to be brusque, even when presented with an opportunity that could help you achieve your aims without suffering that which you find utterly bothersome."

Loathsome was a better word. Shopping for a wife made him itch.

Some of his mother's enthusiasm dimmed. "Should I come with you? I think I sh—"

"*No.*" He didn't let her finish. If she accompanied him, he'd go mad under her attempts to see him betrothed.

She glared at him, but only for a moment. "So dour," she murmured. "Can you at least try to be charming? Perhaps smile a little?"

Smiling was for insincere people. When Dare smiled, he meant it. "Why pretend to be someone

I'm not? My future wife should know precisely whom she's marrying."

His mother exhaled. "That's what I'm afraid of." She paused, rallying her troops once more before she entered the breach. "If you can't be charming, you'll need to be...something. You can't expect to win Lady Marina's hand if you don't engage her somehow."

"I suppose I'll have to dance with her." He detested dancing.

"You could promenade. I'm sure there will be plenty of activities. Perhaps you can go for a ride together."

"That would be acceptable." He would appreciate a wife who enjoyed riding. He imagined her touring the estate with him, speaking to the tenants, and offering assistance and support.

"I'm relieved to hear it."

He shrugged. "Although, being a duke is likely enough to win the chit's—or anyone else's—hand."

His mother stared at him, then took a long drink of madeira, nearly draining the glass. "If that's what you think, you deserve a wife who only wants you for your title."

It seemed the battle this evening would go to his mother.

"I am more than my title," he said quietly, and not without a hint of irritation.

"Of course you are, and I hope you realize it. I also hope you find the woman who breaks through that rigid outer shell you wield so relentlessly. She won't see your title at all, and she'll warm to you, in spite of your efforts to keep her away."

Dare blinked. "I won't do that."

"That's all you do, my darling," she said with a loving glow that slightly melted his hardened exterior. He did keep up a wall, and he liked it. Inside his fortress, things were orderly and expected. He hated mess and emotion and anything surprising. The woman for him would understand that and leave him be.

Perhaps his mother was right—he would hold his duchess apart. Was that so bad? "You are far too sentimental, Mother."

The butler entered and announced that dinner was served. Dare finished his brandy, and his mother did the same with her madeira. After depositing their empty glasses on a table for the butler to sweep away, Dare helped the dowager to her feet and offered his arm.

She placed her hand on his sleeve, and they walked into the dining room as they did every night. Peace settled over him. *Same.*

"I love you, my boy," she whispered just before taking her chair.

That was different. Dare was surprised that he didn't mind.

CHAPTER 2

*J*uno blinked against the bright October
sunlight as she departed the coach and
lifted her face to the sky. When she
turned her head, the façade of Blickton, a pale
stone Palladian house constructed in the last cen-
tury, greeted her with sparkling windows and a
wide open door.

A pair of liveried footmen bustled forth, one to
direct their luggage and another to escort them to
the house where a third footman stood just inside
the door and welcomed them to Blickton. While
Juno and Lady Wetherby took in the grand en-
trance hall, Marina looked at the floor. Perhaps she
found the marble particularly compelling.

The butler led them to where everyone was
gathered in the drawing room. On the way, they
passed a large, inviting library, its shelves over-
flowing with books. Marina stopped and lingered
in the doorway, her gaze hungry as she looked eagerly inside.

"You are not spending time in the library," Lady
Wetherby said firmly. "I forbid it. If I so much as
see you with a book, I'll gather up all the ones

you've hoarded at home and send them to a school."

Marina sent her a mutinous scowl, and Juno could practically hear her mind screaming in objection. Not that Marina would ever voice it aloud.

As they continued to the drawing room, Juno fell back with Marina, walking closely beside her. "We'll find a way to explore the library. Leave it to me," she promised, sending her charge an encouraging smile.

"Thank you," Marina murmured, her gaze meeting Juno's for a brief but gratitude-filled moment.

"Our final guests have arrived!" Lady Cosford exclaimed as they entered the drawing room. "Welcome, Lady Wetherby, Lady Marina, and Mrs. Langton."

Their hostess lowered her voice to address them personally. "I'm so pleased you could come." She turned and beckoned to a dark-haired gentleman with warm hazel eyes. "Cosford, darling, come greet Lady Wetherby and her daughter. And Lady Marina's companion." Lady Cosford directed a smile toward Juno, and she was instantly struck by the unmistakable sensation that she'd met a kindred spirit. Someone with a positive outlook and a strong, determined nature. Juno hoped she was right.

After exchanging pleasantries, their host moved on while Lady Cosford remained. She chatted with Lady Wetherby about their trip, and Juno took the opportunity to scout the landscape.

Scanning the room, Juno immediately located the Duke of Warrington. At least, she was fairly certain that was him. When she'd learned of his attendance and, more importantly, of her employer's desire that her daughter become his duchess, Juno had done what she could to recall his likeness and learn all she could about him.

He was not an exceptionally tall man, but he was muscular and fit, with a very attractive face. Rather, it would be if he weren't scowling. He was in possession of two of the weightiest brows Juno had ever seen. Thick and dark, they commanded his expression, riding low and to the center as he surveyed the assembly. His eyes were also dark, as was his thick thatch of hair. All of him exuded a darkness and sobriety that instantly put Juno on guard. *This* was the man who was supposed to marry her charge?

"Come, let me introduce you to the duke," Lady Cosford said.

She had either noticed Juno's interest in him or was aware of Lady Wetherby's hope for a match. Juno would find out which.

"Thank you," Lady Wetherby responded, and they made their way to the corner, where a rain cloud seemed to be parked over the duke's head.

On the way, Juno whispered into Marina's ear, "Make eye contact with the duke and smile. I know it's difficult since you don't know him, but just remember that he doesn't like social engagements either." She'd focused a great deal on the latter in order to alleviate some of Marina's anxiety.

Lady Cosford came to a halt and smiled into the abyss that was the Duke of Warrington. "Duke, allow me to introduce Lady Wetherby and her daughter, Lady Marina." She pivoted toward Juno. "And this is Lady Marina's companion, Mrs. Langton."

The duke barely looked at Juno, which was fine by her, especially since his attention was entirely on Marina. But his features didn't soften even the barest degree.

Marina dropped into a lovely curtsey, her eyes on the floor as usual. "Pleased to make your acquaintance, Duke."

The duke said nothing in response. He flicked a glance toward Lady Wetherby, who also curtsied. Then he did the same to Juno. Executing a flawless curtsey, Juno gave him her most disarming smile. "How wonderful to meet you, Your Grace. We've so been looking forward to it, haven't we, Marina?" She edged closer to her charge, hoping her presence would give the young woman some much-needed courage.

"Yes." Marina lifted her gaze, but not all the way to his face.

Lady Wetherby frowned slightly at her daughter, and Juno could hear the woman criticizing her later. Leaning close to Marina, Juno whispered more advice. "Mention the weather or our trip. Perhaps ask about his journey?"

Her fingers fidgeting together, Marina stared at the duke's neck. "It's a very fine day."

He stared at her, the creases in his brow, which Juno would wager were ever present, deepening. "I suppose."

How on earth were these two going to make a match? Juno felt an unfamiliar sensation—a thick knot of agitation in her chest.

"It's lovely for October," Lady Cosford said, as if the conversation between the duke and Marina weren't the most awkward thing to have ever occurred. "I'm so pleased as I've planned a picnic for tomorrow. Just down by the lake. It will be splendid!"

Juno very much appreciated the woman's enthusiasm and clear understanding of the situation —these two people needed help. "Oh yes, that will be most delightful," she agreed. "What else do you have planned?"

"I'm sure we'll find out later," the duke cut in, giving Juno a look of savage irritation.

Biting her tongue, Juno redoubled her efforts to win the man over—not for her, for Marina. "Certainly. And I look forward to it."

"Excuse me." The duke took a step to the side and walked around them, making sure not to come too close to Juno. He went to where a footman was dispensing beverages.

"He's quite surly," Marina noted, surprising Juno.

"That's a bit rich coming from you," Lady Wetherby responded, thankfully with humor and not malice.

"Might I have a drink, Mother?" Marina asked, glancing toward a different footman with a tray.

"I could do with some wine or whatever is available." Lady Wetherby linked her arm through her daughter's and they departed, leaving Juno with their hostess.

Juno decided not to mince words. "I take it you are aware of Lady Wetherby's plan for her daughter to become betrothed to the duke?"

"Yes, I had suspected as much and thought I would do what I could to ensure the match." Lady Cosford's sherry-colored gaze moved first to the duke and then to Marina. "They are well suited, don't you think?"

"I, ah, perhaps." Juno should just have agreed, but she couldn't see her sweet charge with someone like the duke. Not that others viewed Marina as "sweet." She appeared aloof and distracted, even sullen. Juno had thought so too when they'd first met, but after a few days, she'd come to know the true Marina. She was inquisitive and intellectual. She just didn't like being around people.

Juno ought not judge the duke too harshly. Perhaps he was the same, and in time, they'd all see that it was indeed an excellent match. Thankfully, they had nearly a week to make that determination.

"I propose we join forces," Lady Cosford said quietly, tipping her head toward Juno's. "The duke has come to find a wife, and Lady Marina is the only unmarried young lady."

"Lady Cosford, did you construct the guest list so that His Grace and Lady Marina are the only ones who *can* make a match?" Juno again saw her potential alignment with Lady Cosford as not only friends but coconspirators.

Lady Cosford let out a gentle laugh. "I may have." She winked at Juno, the fine lines around her eye crinkling. Juno estimated the woman's age to be in her mid to late thirties based on the age of her children, but thought she seemed younger. Perhaps that was due to her buoyant disposition.

"Well, if the duke is here to find a wife, he may want to improve his demeanor," Juno said wryly.

"I understand that is your area of expertise." Lady Cosford looked toward the duke, who was still glowering at everything and everyone. "Perhaps you can coax out the duke's...warmer side."

"If he has one. He's awfully stiff." Juno's mind began to work. She was suddenly invigorated to try to find the duke's gentler nature. And if he didn't have one, well, it was better she discover that now and prevent Marina from making a mistake. "I have an idea that will encourage engagement." She leaned close to Lady Cosford and laid out her plan.

"Marvelous. Let's commence immediately." She

started to turn, then paused. "I think you must call me Cecilia. I do believe we're going to be great friends."

Juno could never have too many of those. "Then you must call me Juno. I look forward to our alliance." She wriggled her brows before adopting a more serious tone. "I need to maneuver myself next to the rigid duke."

"Oh, that name might stick," Cecilia said with a sly smile. "Follow me."

Hopefully, Marina would do her part when it came her turn, because Juno wasn't sure she could position herself next to both people who needed her guidance. Goodness, this was going to be a busy and probably taxing house party. She was quite looking forward to the extra payment she would earn for ensuring this match. She'd be able to take a nice long break between positions, which meant enjoying the holidays in Bath and potentially finding a nice gentleman to keep her warm for the winter. Yes, it would all be worth it.

But first, she had to achieve the impossible.

≈

D are wanted to crawl out of his skin. There were too many bloody people crammed into this drawing room, spacious as it might be. The extensive parkland visible from the wide windows beckoned him outside, where he could escape conversation. And that especially annoying companion whose overwrought charm made him want to leave the house party altogether.

But no. He'd come a great distance to find a wife. At least his potential bride wasn't irritating. She was quiet and seemed as uncomfortable as he felt. This could very well be the perfect match.

He sipped his sherry, thinking it was time to excuse himself from the gathering, when Lady Cosford moved to the center of the room with her husband. Cosford tapped his glass to gain everyone's attention.

A lovely floral scent tinged with orange swirled around him. Turning his head, he realized the vexing companion had moved to stand at his side. She smiled up at him, revealing even, white teeth. Her eyes, green like sage, sparkled as if seeing him were the most wonderful thing that had happened to her all day. Did she look at everyone like that? It was more than disarming. It was thoroughly disconcerting.

"Welcome, everyone," Lord Cosford intoned before glancing at his wife, who stood at his side. "Lady Cosford has a charming activity for us to begin the festivities."

She gave her husband a bright smile. Watching them together made Dare want to roll his eyes. He glanced toward the companion—what was her name?—to find her watching him with interest. He wished she'd go somewhere else.

"Thank you," Lady Cosford said to her husband before addressing the room. "I thought it would be amusing to begin with introductions. We'll go around the room and introduce ourselves, then share something interesting. For example, I would say I'm Lady Cosford and that I enjoy lemon rosemary ices. Let us form a circle around the room— quickly if we can, please."

She bustled toward the doorway with her husband, effectively blocking an escape unless Dare wanted to throw himself through one of the windows. The idea held astonishing appeal. He didn't want to stand in a circle, nor did he want to share a bloody thing.

"Let's just move over here," the companion said cheerily, effectively steering him into the infernal circle without even touching him. How did she do that?

"Lovely," Lady Cosford said, again with another grating smile. "I've already demonstrated how we will go on, but I'll offer another tidbit about myself to spark your enthusiasm." She laughed, and Dare wished he was anywhere else, even a London ballroom. "I like to walk in the rain. Not a downpour, mind you, but a fine mist is quite lovely, especially in the autumn." She looked over at her husband, and they seemed to share a… connection. A speechless moment in which something passed between them. Shockingly, Dare didn't want to roll his eyes. He felt a slight but distinct envy.

Shaking the sensation away, he turned his mind to other matters, namely the renovations occurring at his house in London. He would travel there after this to assess the progress. He was so successful in his distraction that he failed to realize it was his turn.

The woman beside him—the companion of his potential betrothed—nudged him gently with her elbow. "Your turn," she whispered.

Her touch shocked him. No one touched him. Ever. Except when his mother occasionally insisted on hugging him. And his lovers, whenever he decided to take one.

"You're growling," she murmured, drawing him to look at her.

Was he? Frowning, he looked at the expectant circle of people and wondered what in the devil he was doing there. "You all know who I am." He hadn't given any thought to what he might say, nor had he listened to anyone else. So he said the first thing that came to his mind. "I loathe house parties."

The reactions were actually rather entertaining. Two ladies clapped their hands over their mouths, and several gentlemen smirked, while at least one nodded in agreement.

The woman beside him sucked in a breath. Now it was her turn.

"I am Mrs. Langton." She spoke with a warmth and charm that made even Dare want to turn toward her. So he did. "I like to play chess, but I am quite terrible at it." She shot a provoking look at Dare and added, "Also, I *love* house parties. Such a wonderful opportunity to meet new people and have a splendid time."

All Dare could think was that he also enjoyed chess. However, he was an accomplished player, so he couldn't challenge Mrs. Langton—he found himself wondering what her given name was—to a game.

Wait, he wanted to play chess with her and learn her name?

Only because she was beginning to interest him. He was a disagreeable person, and she didn't seem vexed by him in the slightest. She was either very good at hiding her emotions, or she was the most pleasant person in England. Perhaps she was both. Whatever she was, he found her intriguing, and *that* was irritating.

The person next to her continued, and Dare forced himself to look away from Mrs. Langton. She was stunningly attractive, he realized. Petite with a rather intricate hairstyle, and she wore the very latest fashion. He only knew that because his mother enjoyed poring over plates and sharing her favorite styles with him when he visited her at the dower house. Because of this, he could see that

Mrs. Langton was quite well turned out for a young lady's companion. Perhaps there was more to her than met the eye.

Detecting the mischief lurking in her cheerful expression, he could believe that rather easily.

He spent the remainder of the interminable exercise contemplating the woman beside him. How had she come to be Lady Marina's companion? Was she from a wealthy family? That would explain her clothing. Was she truly a missus, as in a widow, or had she adopted the title as part of her employment?

By the time Lord Cosford, who was thankfully the last person in the circle, spoke, Dare was thoroughly annoyed with himself for spending so much time thinking of Mrs. Langton. He would deal with her as she pertained to the woman he was considering as his wife. Speaking of...he'd entirely missed whatever she'd said.

"That was most informative," Lady Cosford said. "Now, we shall have a respite before dinner is served at half six. Following dinner this evening, we'll have dancing and games. Tomorrow we'll picnic by the lake. It will be such fun!" She was nearly as ebullient as Mrs. Langton.

Dare glanced toward the latter woman to find her again studying him. Just as her touch had discomfited him, he felt off-balance under her regard.

"I play chess," he blurted.

"Do you? Perhaps you can help me improve my game."

He would say she was flirting, but a young lady's companion wouldn't do that. Which meant she was simply earnest in her desire to improve her chess. Didn't it?

Oh, he didn't like this sort of nonsense one bit. It was past time to beat a hasty retreat and do whatever possible to avoid Mrs. Langton for the duration of the house party. He didn't feel particularly optimistic since she'd be fixed to Lady Marina's side. Although, she wasn't at present...

"I do hope we'll see you here before dinner. May I suggest you escort Lady Marina into the dining room?"

What a brazen woman. But he supposed that was her job—to push her charge at him. He couldn't decide if a companion was worse than a managing mother. Since Lady Marina had both, he could count himself unfortunate.

"I would be honored," he said, his muscles screaming to spring for the doorway, which Lord and Lady Cosford had thankfully removed themselves from. Others were leaving, which meant he could too.

Without further comment, he strode away from her and left the drawing room, taking deep breaths as if the air were somehow clearer and his lungs less compressed now that he was away from everyone. Several footmen stood ready to show guests to their rooms because everyone had come directly to the drawing room upon arrival.

Dare eagerly found someone to lead him to his chamber, a sprawling suite in the northwest corner of the first floor overlooking the parkland as well as some of the front drive. It was a pleasing view and blissfully devoid of anyone save himself and the footman, who was even now departing.

His solitude was short-lived, for his valet, Chadwick, came from the adjoining dressing chamber. "Would you care to rest before dinner, or will you be taking a walk on the estate?"

Dare shot his valet, who'd been with him a decade, a grateful look. "Most definitely a walk. It was too long in a coach today and then cooped up inside with an excess of people."

"I have your clothing laid out in the dressing chamber already." Chadwick inclined his balding blond head.

"You are most efficient," Dare said.

"I aim to be, Your Grace." He turned on his heel and went back into the dressing chamber.

Eager to get outside, Dare followed him. He could hardly wait to clear his mind of all the nonsense from today and brace himself for that which was to come.

CHAPTER 3

"They make a lovely couple," Cecilia noted as she and Juno watched Marina dance with the duke. "Their hair color, like their personalities, is a perfect match."

Juno still wasn't convinced their personalities were suited. Yes, they were both somewhat quiet, but Marina didn't possess the duke's...rigidity. Or contrariness. She would never declare that she hated something out loud, let alone in front of two dozen or so other people. And she would certainly never insult her hostess.

"Did it bother you when His Grace said he hated house parties?" Juno asked.

Cecilia waved her hand, laughing. "Goodness, no. His reputation as a disagreeable gentleman is well known. Honestly, I find his candor refreshing amongst our class."

That was one way to look at him. Juno had to agree he and Marina made a nice couple, at least visually. Perhaps it was their serious, concentrated expressions. They could actually be bookends, she decided.

"I do appreciate your clever seating arrangement at dinner." Juno was pleased that she and the duke had flanked Marina. That allowed Juno to support and advise her charge—which she'd done in the barest of whispers—while Marina and the duke could get to know each other. However, as Cecilia had noted, they were both quiet people. Juno feared they wouldn't converse enough to determine if they would suit. But perhaps that wouldn't be necessary. It was possible the duke had already decided whether he would propose.

Juno hoped that wasn't the case. She preferred they took some time, a few days at least, to get to know one another, to be sure of the match. Lady Wetherby didn't care about that—she just wanted a proposal. Thankfully, she'd been seated away from them at dinner, which had put Marina more at ease. She'd even smiled at the duke. Once.

"I am more than happy to help." Cecilia turned toward her, lowering her voice. "In fact, I've arranged for her and Rigid"—her lip twitched, and Juno nearly laughed—"to share a picnic blanket tomorrow—along with you and Lady Wetherby, of course. Mr. and Mrs. Teasmore will join you. The blankets are large enough for six, with a footman assigned to each."

"That sounds lovely. I will endeavor to ensure Rigid and Marina walk to the picnic location together."

Cecilia gave her a fervent nod. "And I shall do my best to assist."

A gasp, along with a chorus of voices, sounded from where the furniture had been cleared for dancing on the other side of the room. The music, provided by Cecilia's oldest daughter, who was fifteen, on the pianoforte, stopped.

Juno and Cecilia whipped their attention toward the commotion. A puddle of pale yellow silk surrounded Marina where she sat on the floor.

Lady Wetherby was already rushing to her, while the duke helped Marina to her feet.

"Did you see what happened?" Cecilia asked.

"I didn't." Juno had been too focused on their conversation.

"Oh, look," Cecilia breathed, staring at the duke as he gently helped Marina find her footing. Then he offered his arm and escorted her to a chair. He bent his head and spoke to her before moving toward the refreshment table.

"Lovely," Juno murmured. Perhaps this match would work after all.

The duke returned with a glass of ratafia, which he handed to Marina. She accepted the drink, then darted a look toward Juno. Her eyes were wider than normal, and her forehead creased. Juno had seen that expression before. Marina needed help.

"Pardon me," Juno said before going to join her charge.

Lady Wetherby took a chair next to Marina's. The duke stood nearby. Cecilia's daughter began playing and the dancing resumed, minus Marina and the duke, of course.

"What on earth happened?" Lady Wetherby asked Marina.

"It was my fault," the duke said gruffly.

Marina briefly lifted her gaze to his. Juno knew in that moment that the duke had lied, that he'd covered for Marina. Perhaps he wasn't so unlikable.

"I'm sure it wasn't," Lady Wetherby said with a smile. She turned her attention to her daughter. "All right, then, Marina? Ready to rejoin the dance?"

"I hurt my ankle, Mother," Marina said quietly. Again, she sent a pleading look toward Juno.

The duke bowed toward Marina. "I'll let you recuperate."

Juno noted Lady Wetherby's slight frown as she watched him leave. "What a lovely evening it's been," she said brightly. While it may not have ended the way the countess wanted, dinner had been a success, as had been the duke's concern following the dancing mishap. Juno bent her head to say, "It seems great progress was made, my lady."

Lady Wetherby pursed her lips. "We shall see."

"I would like to retire," Marina said, rising slowly to her feet.

Juno provided assistance, for Marina did seem a tad wobbly. "I'll take you upstairs."

"I'm going to remain here." Lady Wetherby looked up at Marina. "I hope your ankle is better by morning."

"I'm sure it will be." Marina took Juno's arm, and they started toward the door.

Juno directed a sympathetic look toward Cecilia, silently indicating all was well. Cecilia responded with a slight nod. Tomorrow at the picnic, they'd do what they could to encourage the burgeoning connection between Marina and the duke.

As they left the drawing room, Marina moved slowly, and Juno was genuinely concerned about her ankle. "Are you terribly hurt?"

Marina straightened and took her hand from Juno's arm. "No. I just wanted to leave." She gave Juno a sheepish look.

"I understand you find these sorts of gatherings difficult, and after you wed, you may be able to avoid them entirely. In fact, if you wed the duke, I suspect that will be what you both prefer."

"It isn't just that," Marina said. "I completely forgot the steps of the dance and collided with the duke. It wasn't his fault at all." Red flagged her cheeks, and Juno patted her shoulder.

"Don't be embarrassed. That sort of thing happens to everyone at some point or another."

"I can't imagine it ever happens to you." Marina allowed one of her rare smiles. "You're so perfect."

Juno laughed. "Hardly. I met Mr. Langton at an assembly, and I spilled punch on him."

Marina actually giggled. "You have to be making that up."

"I swear I am not." Juno noted they were near the library. "Come, let's get you a book or four since your mother's not around." She glanced back toward the drawing room, but knew the countess would stay as long as the wine was flowing. Then she'd retire to her chamber, which was directly next to the one Juno was sharing with Marina. She'd never know her daughter had been to the library.

Fortunately, the room was empty of people. It was, however, well lit with a cheery fire burning in the large fireplace. Juno browsed the shelves as Marina plucked books and flipped through them. She stacked one then another on a table before moving across the room to continue her search. Another tome landed on another table.

Juno liked seeing Marina's enthusiasm and wished it extended beyond books. Alas, Marina would be quite happy to closet herself in a room such as this and perhaps not emerge for months, even years. It was too bad she had such high expectations, but that was the position into which she'd been born. Juno somewhat understood what that felt like. As the granddaughter of a baron, she'd been expected to marry a country gentleman, not a dashing scholar who'd just taken a position as headmaster of a school.

Her parents had refused to endorse their marriage, and Juno hadn't seen them since—nearly eight years ago. She liked to think they'd be proud of the life she'd built for herself. Juno certainly was. Indeed, she had everything she could hope for: respectability, comfort, and independence. And she didn't have to answer to a man or parents.

"I'm ready."

Juno blinked, lost briefly in her reverie. Marina stood before her clutching five, no six, books.

"Are those just for tonight or for the duration of our stay?" Juno quipped.

"Oh, they won't last as long as we'll be here. Unless we get to leave early," Marina said eagerly.

"I doubt that," Juno said as they left. The only way that would happen was if Marina became betrothed to the duke. Which *could* happen if the duke was decisive. That trait certainly seemed to fit his demeanor. She couldn't imagine he was one to dither.

As they climbed the stairs, Juno asked if Marina liked the duke.

"It's too early to say," Marina demurred.

"It was nice of him to attend you after the incident on the dance floor."

"It was." Marina hugged the books more tightly to her chest as they reached the top of the stairs. "That was particularly kind. I admit I was surprised. He seems so dour."

"I suspect that outward crustiness covers a soft, sweet inside." Juno hoped it did. If not, she would feel rather bad for him.

"You make him sound like a food. Perhaps a confection."

"You are not unlike that," Juno said softly. "Your exterior does not always reveal who you truly are."

Marina exhaled. "I know. I do try. It's just so

hard to feel comfortable around people when I'd much rather be by myself. Not all the time, mind you. I do enjoy your company."

"You didn't at first," Juno recalled with a laugh as they approached their chamber. "I distinctly remember you glowering at me for at least three days."

Marina gave her another sheepish look. "I was angry at my mother for hiring you. I didn't want 'refinement.' I took that out on you, and I'm sorry."

Juno opened the door and motioned for Marina to precede her inside. "There is no need to apologize. I am used to young ladies not always welcoming me with glee." Why would they when Juno was brought in to fix a disastrous or near-disastrous situation?

Marina went to deposit her books on the table next to her side of the bed. "I shall need to hide these in case Mother stops in later." She frowned at the stack, then muttered something.

"Is there something amiss?" Juno asked as she removed an earring and set it on the dresser.

"I left one of the books downstairs." Marina's brow pleated in disappointment. "Naturally, that was the one I wanted to read first."

Juno knew the effort Marina was putting into meeting her mother's expectations and wanted to ease her stress. "I'll run down and get it."

"You don't have to do that," Marina said earnestly. "I can make do. I daresay I have plenty to read." Her cheeks flushed as she glanced toward the pile of books.

"I don't mind. Truly," Juno assured her.

"You are most kind," Marina said gratefully. "It's on the table near the windows at the back."

Flashing Marina a smile and a wave of her fingers, Juno hastily departed, hurrying back downstairs lest an enterprising maid or footman replace the book on the shelf before Juno arrived. The library was no longer empty, however. Standing over the table Marina had indicated was none other than the Duke of Warrington.

He turned toward Juno as she approached.

"Good evening, Your Grace," she said. "I see you've found my book."

Picking up the book, he opened the cover and flipped a few pages. "You're going to read about butterflies?"

"No, actually. It's for Lady Marina. Although, I suppose I might find butterflies interesting." Juno mostly read magazines and news. She liked to know what was going on in the world as well as the latest fashions. "Lady Marina is exceptionally well read." Some gentlemen would find that irksome, but she suspected the duke would not.

His eyes glimmered with curiosity, and Juno was pleased to see she was right. "Are butterflies a particular interest?"

"I'm not certain. She typically reads whatever she can lay her hands on." Juno clasped her hands in front of her waist. "You and she seemed to get on quite well at dinner."

"Are you playing matchmaker, Mrs. Langton?" From another gentleman, it might have been a flirtatious comment, but from the duke, it was accusatory. Or perhaps it only seemed that way because of his infernal eyebrows. Thick and dark, they were magnificently expressive. Discerning. Commanding. Captivating.

What? *No.*

Juno blinked. "I was hired to ensure Lady Marina is successful on the Marriage Mart. If that makes me a matchmaker, then I suppose I am."

"You are more than an ordinary companion,

then." He scrutinized her, his dark eyes moving in a languid perusal. "How *ex*traordinary." The last came out in a low, rough murmur, but then everything he said sounded as if he'd swallowed darkness. She couldn't say she disliked it. In fact, it was impossible not to rivet her attention to his every word.

Except she refused to do that. Or at least, allow him to realize she was. No man was ever going to wield a seductive power over her ever again. She was the provocative one now, and she was very, *very* selective.

"You seemed to enjoy Lady Marina's company," Juno said, focusing on the only thing that mattered —matching him with Marina.

"She's quiet and pleasant."

"Marina—Lady Marina—also enjoyed herself." Juno purposely used her name, hoping the duke might begin to think of her in more intimate terms.

"Did that include the dance?"

Was that a bit of humor in his voice? Juno couldn't help but smile. This match *could* work. "It did not. I'm afraid Marina is not terribly fond of dancing, even when it all goes well. I hope that doesn't trouble you."

"Not at all. In fact, I count that as a mark in her favor. I loathe dancing."

"You dislike a great many things, it seems," Juno said, not without a touch of sarcasm.

"I see no point in pretending to enjoy things I do not. If I said I liked house parties, I'd be invited to a plethora. If I pretended to love dancing, I'd be expected to gallivant across every dance floor. It's best to set accurate expectations, don't you agree?"

Juno found it hard to argue with that. "I admit I find your candor refreshing, if bemusing."

"You'll get used to it. Or not. I expect our acquaintance will be rather short-lived."

He was right. Whether he wed Marina or not, Juno would move on to her next client after her well-earned respite over the holidays.

His hand lifted, and he reached for her ear. She froze, expecting his touch. But it didn't come. He lowered his arm. "You're missing an earring. Did you lose it?"

She brought her fingers to her earlobe. "No, I removed it upstairs."

"I was going to offer to help you find it."

Was he? He was an odd gentleman. "What *do* you like, Your Grace?"

He hesitated, one brow moving higher than the other. "Riding. Walking. Being outside. Reading. Chess." His gaze moved toward a board on a small table flanked by two chairs.

Juno stored that information away, then redirected their conversation lest she continue finding him interesting. There was no point in that. "Marina appreciated your kindness after the dancing mishap."

His lip twitched, and he glanced away. Juno could have sworn he'd made a soft growl in his throat, but she had to be hearing things.

"It wasn't a kindness," he rumbled.

"Whether you meant it as such, it was exactly that." She wondered if compliments made him uncomfortable. Her mother was like that.

"Here." He handed her the book, and their fingers grazed as she took it from him.

A flash of heat danced up her arm. She jerked her gaze to his, surprised to find him looking at her with an intensity that matched the warmth suddenly taking over her body.

"Thank you. Good night." She spun about and

hurried from the library, irritated with herself for not discussing tomorrow's picnic with him. He said he liked setting expectations. She should have told him they would all be sitting together. So he could anticipate it.

She was going to try her best to do the opposite.

~

*A*fter an exhilarating early morning ride on one of Cosford's finest mounts, Dare was feeling quite fine and fit. He was even looking forward to the picnic. Any entertainment that could be undertaken outside was instantly more desirable.

In fact, he was so eager that he left before thinking to accompany Lady Marina and her companion. He stood gazing out at the lake from the picnic area when the other guests began to arrive.

Lady Marina, her mother, and Mrs. Langton arrived in the middle of the pack. Dare's attention went first to the companion, positioned between the other two women. She was shorter than they were, her form more petite. Again, she wore a sleek costume that seemed beyond her station. She looked like a member of the family, not a paid employee. Except her blonde hair and green eyes, as well as her stature, were at odds with the dark hair and blue eyes of the taller Fellowes women.

As usual, Mrs. Langton wore a bright smile and seemed to be on the verge of laughter. If he had to describe her, he'd say she was perpetually delighted. He found it vastly irritating, but also intriguing. He ought to pay closer attention to Lady Marina. She wasn't irritating—or delighted—at all. She was reserved and reticent, the perfect companion for him. She wouldn't provoke him to smile, or nearly so, or hurl compliments at him.

Nevertheless, he found himself wanting to know more about Mrs. Langton. How had she come to be an *extraordinary* companion who dressed as if she managed Society with one hand? She radiated confidence and charm. She was the kind of woman a normal duke—one who cared about appearances and social dominance—would want. Except she was a paid companion.

Why in the hell was he still thinking about her?

Dare refocused his attention on his potential bride. He was so intent that he failed to notice his hostess had approached him.

"Duke, may I show you to your blanket?" she asked with a bothersome smile. But then, were there any other kind? He supposed genuine ones were all right. Problem was, there were really so few of them. "I've seated you with Lady Marina."

Of course she had. He almost asked if everyone in attendance, including the retainers, was part of the matchmaking, but held his tongue. Perhaps he didn't need to say everything he was thinking, even if he did think it was helpful to be perfectly candid.

He simply said, "Thank you" and allowed Lady Cosford to lead him to the blanket where Lady Marina and her entourage were already taking their seats on artfully arranged pillows.

Frowning at his pillow, Dare moved it out of the way so he could sit beside Lady Marina. Mrs. Langton was situated behind them, while Lady Wetherby was on the other side of her daughter. Good. Hopefully she wouldn't try to speak to Dare around Lady Marina. He'd already decided she was a pain in the arse.

Another couple joined their blanket, and Dare

didn't bother to remember who they were. He was here to find a wife, not make social connections.

"Good afternoon," he said, initiating conversation with Lady Marina.

She barely met his gaze. "Good afternoon."

Did she make eye contact with anyone besides her mother and Mrs. Langton? Dare didn't think so, but perhaps he wasn't paying close enough attention. It was too bad she had such a distracting companion. She would do far better with a doddering aunt who wore lace mobcaps and fell asleep in her sherry. Someone who wasn't pretty or engaging. Or whose touch caused an alarming sense of...*oh hell.*

He almost asked Lady Marina about the butterfly book, but then he'd have to explain how he knew of its existence. Which meant he'd have to reveal that he'd met Mrs. Langton in the library last night. And what would be wrong with that? It hadn't been scandalous.

Why did it feel that way, then?

"I enjoy being outdoors," he said, disrupting the troubling direction of his thoughts. "Do you?"

"I suppose. I enjoy quiet."

"You'd prefer if you were alone on this blanket."

Her gaze shot to his, but only briefly. "Perhaps." She'd hesitated as if she'd wanted to say yes, but decided it wasn't right.

"Alone on this blanket and without all the other blankets, I'd wager. If I were a betting man, which I most certainly am not." He didn't like things that were unexpected or left to chance. All his investments were conservative and sound, and he didn't so much as enter a gaming room.

He thought she might respond, and when she did not, he fell into silence. He wasn't going to work overly hard to engage her. Why should he if they were both comfortable with mutual quietude?

As beverages were distributed, Dare nearly spilled his wine when Mrs. Langton leaned closer behind him. "You should ask her to promenade," she whispered. "She's shy, but if it's the two of you alone, she will relax. Then you can become better acquainted."

A shiver dashed across the back of Dare's neck. Mrs. Langton's fruity, floral scent overtook his senses. He took a fortifying drink of wine.

He didn't particularly want to promenade with Lady Marina, but he supposed he must. If she was to be his wife, they had to get to know one another. It wasn't as if they'd live their life in silence. Could they?

Turning his head, he asked Lady Marina if she cared to promenade. A footman took his wineglass.

Lady Marina looked toward her mother, who in turn glanced at Mrs. Langton. "Take Juno with you," Lady Wetherby said.

Juno. Had she been named after the goddess?

Dare helped Lady Marina to her feet, then pivoted to perform the same service for her companion. Mrs. Langton's sage eyes met his, and he knew she wasn't being purposely provocative, but damn if he didn't want to dive right into their green depths.

Frowning, he turned his back to her and offered Lady Marina his arm. They strolled from the blanket toward the lake. He felt unsettled, agitated. Because of the goddess.

He forced his attention to being in his favorite place: outside. It was a fine October day—the morning had been cool and damp, and this afternoon was warm and bright. The trees were not yet at their peak colors, but already they flashed gold and orange. Inhaling deeply, Dare got a nose full of Mrs. Langton's distinctive, delicious fragrance. He scowled.

Lady Marina broke the silence, but Dare hadn't been paying attention. "Pardon?" he barked.

She hesitated. "Might we slow down a bit?"

Was he going too fast? He didn't think so. Still, he decreased his pace until he felt as if he were walking through a swiftly moving stream.

"Thank you," she murmured.

"I like to walk quickly. I enjoy a long, robust constitutional most days."

"I prefer a more sedate pace."

"I can see that." His mother would say he was being terse. However, he couldn't help who he was or the fact that he preferred to speak without censoring himself. His future wife needed to understand and accept that.

They'd reached the lake, a small but pretty spot of blue surrounded by flowers and greenery and in one area, a muddy beach. That would be an excellent location to enter the water for a refreshing swim, which sounded quite pleasant. If it was an activity to be done outside, Dare enjoyed it.

"Oh!" Lady Marina took her hand from his arm and danced away, waving her arms madly.

He watched her in dismay. "What the devil is wrong with you?"

"There's a bee!"

"It won't hurt you," he said calmly. "The more you move, the more you'll agitate it."

She continued to flail her arms as her hat became dislodged. She was also moving precariously close to the edge of the lake.

"Careful," he warned, reaching for her just as Mrs. Langton moved between her charge and the water. Dare's hand collided with the goddess's shoulder, and she fell straight back into the lake.

"Christ!" Dare didn't think twice before launching himself in after her.

Thankfully, the water wasn't deep, and he quickly found his footing, his boots squishing into the muddy bottom. The goddess slapped her hands in and out of the water as she struggled to stand. It had to be much harder in a gown.

Dare swept her up into his arms out of the water. "All right?"

"I don't swim."

"I do. Perhaps you should learn."

"If that was an offer of instruction, I think I'll pass. I can't imagine you'd be a pleasant teacher."

Her words struck him like a stone.

"Nevertheless, I am glad you swim so that you could rescue me," she said.

"Swimming wasn't required. The water here doesn't even reach my waist." Cradling her in his arms, he lifted her onto the bank amidst a patch of now-crushed daisies.

She wobbled slightly on her feet, but found her balance. Looking down at herself, she laughed. "Good heavens, I'm a mess."

Her laughter shocked him. He expected annoyance or upset but not *humor*. A smile tried to tug at his mouth, so he deepened his frown.

Lady Marina took her companion's hand and pulled her away from the lake. "I'm so sorry, Juno!"

Juno. Dare would never tire of hearing that name. In fact, he refused to think of her as anything else from now on. He pulled himself onto the bank and straightened, water dripping from every part of him, particularly his hair. He reached up and patted the top of his head, realizing he'd lost his hat.

Looking toward Juno, he nearly lost his breath too. Her gown was plastered to her petite, but incredibly shapely, form. The image left little to his imagination. Actually, it gave him all sorts of ideas. His body was already moving in that direction. He swore violently, and as the two women jerked their attention toward him, he realized he'd done so loudly enough that they could hear him. He swore again but silently this time.

"Mrs. Langton." A footman handed her a blanket, which she wrapped around herself.

"Are you all right?" Lady Cosford asked, having arrived just behind the footman. Lady Wetherby was following, but still had a few yards to go.

The goddess tried to adjust her hat, which was hanging askew from her head. "Just wet."

"We must thank the duke," Lady Cosford noted, looking toward him with gratitude.

"I suppose so," Juno murmured as she sent him a stunning glower that should have eviscerated him. Instead, he felt strangely and wonderfully *alive*.

And if that wasn't absolutely terrible, he didn't know what was.

"I'll walk back to the house with you," Lady Marina offered in her timid voice as she put her hand on her companion's arm.

"You can't go back," Lady Wetherby said, appearing winded as she drew sharp, fast breaths.

"I'm sure the duke must also return to the house, Mother," Lady Marina snapped in a rare display of emotion.

Juno looked upon her with a glow of admiration. "I need to get out of these wet clothes."

Dare nearly groaned at the thought.

Lady Marina and the goddess—she could be Aphrodite now, he realized a bit absurdly—started toward the house, but not before Juno sent him another perturbed glance. She was annoyed with him, and why shouldn't she be? He'd knocked her into the lake in the first place. He owed her an apology. Yes, he'd make sure to do that later.

First, he needed to get out of his wet clothes. And probably make use of his hand lest he spend the rest of the day with a towering erection.

CHAPTER 4

*J*uno had emerged from the lake smelling like a pair of boots that had sat outside in the rain for a week. Perhaps a month. She felt much better after a warm, fragranced bath. She felt better physically, anyway. Mentally, she was still angry with the duke. Not because he'd accidentally pushed her into the lake, but because he'd behaved like an obnoxious boor while promenading with Marina.

There was simply no way Juno could support a match between her charge and the Rigid Duke. And now she needed to convey that to Lady Wetherby.

Squaring her shoulders, she marched to the countess's chamber and knocked on the door, hoping she wasn't disturbing the woman's predinner toilette. Her maid answered and admitted her inside. Lady Wetherby sat with her hair half-styled.

"You're dry," Lady Wetherby said. Was she surprised that Juno had cleaned up after falling into the lake? "What a mess that was, ruining Marina's picnic."

Juno gave her head a light shake. The countess

could be rather difficult to track. "Yes, it was quite frustrating, but I suppose we have the duke to blame for that." Juno was not above pointing out that he'd been the one to cause the "mess."

"Why would we blame him?" Lady Wetherby waved her hand as the maid returned to styling her hair for dinner. "Oh, he knocked you in, didn't he? I heard mention of that." It seemed an afterthought to her.

"Yes. That was after he was quite uncharitable to Marina when she was being harassed by a bee." Marina had been stung several times a few years ago—a story she'd related after they'd had a similar encounter with a bee last month—and was deathly afraid of them.

"Goodness, Marina needs to stiffen up. She was stung a few times and recovered quite well. That girl is stronger than she thinks."

Juno blinked. While she didn't always agree with Lady Wetherby's demeanor toward her daughter, it was moments like this that reminded Juno of two things: the countess didn't have a poor opinion of Marina, and she knew her far better than Juno did.

Moving closer to where Lady Wetherby sat, Juno changed her approach. "I wanted to speak with you about this proposed match. I'm not at all sure it's working out."

Lady Wetherby narrowed her eyes. "It's only been a day, Mrs. Langton."

"While that's true, I just can't see how it's a good match. Marina and the duke are far too alike. With both of them being so…guarded, one wonders how they will get on—not just with each other but in Society. Though it's difficult to tell, neither seems very interested in the other. Furthermore, His Grace was quite rude to Marina while they walked today. She deserves a husband who will treat her with respect and be a supportive partner."

"He possesses a gruff nature," Lady Wetherby said dismissively. "The fact that they are so alike is why they are a perfect match. From what I can tell, they'll sit in companionable silence and won't trouble each other at all. Honestly, that sounds like a splendid marriage indeed. Especially for Marina."

Again, Juno blinked at her employer. Perhaps she was right. Juno didn't like the duke—well, she didn't like his treatment of Marina—and she was allowing her emotions to cloud her judgment. She should talk to Marina and see if she was still open to marrying him. Was he even considering proposing? Given his behavior that afternoon, it might be that he didn't care to wed Marina.

Which was shortsighted on his part. Marina was lovely—smart, kind, and capable of running a household. Probably. Her mother was right that Marina was stronger than she realized. Juno would remind her of that at every possible opportunity.

"Do not be concerned that there doesn't appear to be a spark between them either," Lady Wetherby said. "Most marriages don't begin with such rubbish."

While Juno had enjoyed quite a spark with Bernard, she'd learned it shouldn't be the primary objective in a marriage. Still, it was important. "I would hate for Marina to be unhappy."

"Her happiness isn't your goal—her marriage is." Lady Wetherby exhaled. "I don't mean to sound uncaring, and I do appreciate your concern for Marina, but she will manage. You must agree that a man like the duke would be much better for her than someone else. Someone who, say, enjoys conversing."

While it sounded insulting, the countess wasn't

wrong. She knew her daughter and her discomfort with people she didn't know. Even when Marina did get to know someone, she could be rather reserved.

"I expect them to marry, Mrs. Langton." Lady Wetherby directed a demanding stare toward Juno. "Remember that I have given you a rather large incentive. I would hate to be disappointed, particularly when I must write a recommendation for your next position."

Juno rarely felt disgruntled with people, but Lady Wetherby was trying her typically pleasant nature. "I shall do my best with what I have. We shall have to hope His Grace will loosen up a trifle."

Lady Wetherby turned her attention from Juno, giving the impression she was dismissed. Turning, Juno departed the room and went in search of her ally in this matchmaking challenge.

After finally asking a footman, Juno met with Cecilia in the dining room, where she was overseeing the final arrangements for that evening. "Oh, Juno, I'm so glad to see you're recovered from your earlier mishap." Cecilia walked around the table to join her.

"I am, thank you. It was a rather chilling event," she quipped.

"You seemed perturbed about it, and I'm just so sorry it happened."

"I was annoyed with Rigid. He treated Marina rather obnoxiously during their promenade. She is justifiably afraid of bees and was being harassed by one. He had no sympathy for her situation."

Cecilia's brow pinched. "That doesn't sound promising."

"Not at all. I went to see Lady Wetherby to inform her that I didn't think they would suit. She insists they are perfect for one another and expects them to wed." Juno pressed two fingers to her temple. "This is going to be more difficult than I imagined."

"I see." Cecilia glanced toward the table. "I have placed them next to each other again, with you beside Lady Marina as you were last night."

"I wonder if I ought to sit next to Rigid and try to encourage him to behave more politely. If he continues to act poorly with Marina, she will never relax around him. And if that happens, I can't see him proposing marriage."

"Unless he likes that about her. He's rather... reserved himself."

"I think you mean rigid." Juno winked at her. "In truth, after listening to him speak with Marina during their promenade, I began to doubt his interest in her. Yes, I think I must sit next to him to prod him along."

"I'll make the change," Cecilia said. "Tomorrow there will be a treasure hunt. The guests will be divided into teams to search for items on a list, and the winning team will receive a prize. I have made the duke, Lady Marina, and you a team."

This would provide ample opportunity to determine if they would suit. "Splendid. I'm sure I can find an excuse to leave them alone at some point."

Cecilia's eyes gleamed with intent. "I'll do what I can to help."

"You are an excellent accomplice."

"It seems, ah, very important that this match happens. I will do whatever I can."

"I appreciate your support. Together, I can't imagine we won't be successful."

Cecilia laughed softly. "How I wish I had met you before now. How old are you anyway?"

"Twenty-seven."

"And what happened to Mr. Langton, if you don't mind my nosiness."

"I don't mind at all. He died very suddenly within a year of our marriage." Juno felt a moment's sting as she recalled his senseless demise. Bernard was lovely but also foolish, and he drank too much.

"You seem to have landed on your feet. Do you have as many lives as a cat?"

Now Juno laughed. "Not yet, but I shall hope so. I have been very fortunate to establish myself."

"You seem perfectly suited for your chosen profession. I take it you have no desire to marry again?"

"None whatsoever." Juno had no need or inclination.

"Not even for male companionship?"

"Marriage isn't necessary for that," Juno whispered with a smile.

"How enterprising of you." Cecilia tipped her head toward Juno. "Do you have a specific tactic in mind for how you will encourage the duke's enthusiasm toward Lady Marina?"

"Not entirely. Perhaps he simply needs to be reminded that he came here to find a wife, and Marina is his only option." Juno winced inwardly. She didn't like thinking of Marina in that way. She deserved better than that. "He needs to give her—them—a true chance." Juno was still dubious. Perhaps he was too, which put them in agreement. She marveled at that for a moment.

"Are you talking about me?"

The gruff sound of the duke's voice prompted both Juno and Cecilia to whip around and face the door. The rigid duke stood just inside the dining room, his perpetual scowl only slightly less etched into his face than usual.

"Yes," Juno answered quickly, drawing a sharp glance from Cecilia.

The duke stared at her a moment. Juno heard Cecilia's breath catch.

He shrugged. "I was just passing."

"I must be off," Cecilia said. "I've much to do." She looked toward Juno with slightly widened eyes, her head tilting infinitesimally toward the duke in silent communication that Juno should speak with him. Or something.

The duke stepped out of the way as Cecilia departed.

"I imagine she's planning another tedious event for the morrow." His mouth slashed into a frown as his thick brows gathered.

Juno had suffered enough of his eternal disdain. Moving toward him, she threw her shoulders back and puffed up her chest as she sought to mimic him. "I hate house parties and picnics, and I'm the grumpiest man alive." She pouted up at him, then bared her teeth, lowering her voice even more to a harsh rasp. "But I'm a duke, so I can behave like an ass and get away with it."

His eyes rounded. He opened his mouth, then clamped it shut. "I don't sound like that."

"You sound *exactly* like that." Juno relaxed her shoulders.

"I don't say things like that. The ass part. I know I said I hated house parties."

"Just because you haven't yet said the ass part doesn't mean you won't."

"You think you know me so well?"

"I think you're a shallow, predictable, surly curmudgeon. Perhaps you're more than that, but you won't let anyone see." She adopted her best rigid-duke growl. "I don't need to be pleasant or kind, so I won't. Not even to woo a wife." She stared at him with as much disdain as she could muster, then rolled her eyes for good measure. Satisfied that she felt better even if he never understood her point, she stepped around him to leave.

"That was actually pretty good," he murmured from behind her as she sailed from the dining room.

There was a note of appreciation in his tone that gave her hope. Perhaps tonight would go better than the promenade at the picnic. If it didn't, she wasn't sure the match would happen, regardless of Lady Wetherby's insistence.

～

*D*are wasn't surprised to find himself seated next to Lady Marina again at dinner that evening. However, he was rather speechless—and not because he chose to remain stoic, which was typical—when Mrs. Langton sat on his other side. Still, the first course nearly passed in complete silence among them.

"Why aren't you speaking with Lady Marina?" Mrs. Langton's urgent whisper caught him off guard.

He turned his head to find she was much closer than he'd realized. She'd leaned toward him to deliver her query.

"She's quite focused on her soup," he murmured in response. A glance toward Lady Marina reaffirmed his assessment. She'd yet to make eye contact with him at all and had barely uttered good evening when she'd sat down.

"Don't take her shyness for disinterest," Mrs. Langton said brightly, still keeping her voice low.

She looked at him expectantly, a smile hovering about her lush, kissable mouth.

Kissable?

Dare cleared his throat and snapped his attention back to his soup. A moment later, he tried to engage Lady Marina. "How do you find the turtle soup?"

"Tolerable." Her gaze didn't so much as flick toward his. Or anywhere except her soup.

Frowning, he set down his spoon and pondered whether it was worth his time to bother trying again.

"You could ask her about the wine," Mrs. Langton suggested.

"What about it?" he asked in a low growl.

"You aren't very adept at conversation, are you?"

He couldn't help shooting her a suffering glance. "No worse than your charge."

"She's *shy*." Mrs. Langton blinked, her long lashes shuttering her eyes briefly. "Are you?"

"No. I merely prefer not to engage with most people."

"And why is that?"

"Because I rarely meet anyone worth speaking with."

She exhaled. "Not shy but boorish. Are you looking for a duchess or not? Ask her about the wine," she prodded.

The footman removed the course, and while they laid the next, Dare tried again. Turning his head toward Lady Marina, he willed her to look at him. Did he think he was some sort of sorcerer that he could control her movements? He turned a snort into another growl. Unintentionally, that had the effect of provoking her to glance at him.

"Is the wine to your liking?" he asked, thinking

this had to be the dullest, most painful, most inane conversation he'd ever had. No, it wasn't even a conversation since she wasn't participating.

"I can't say."

"Haven't you tried it?"

"No." She reached for her glass and took a delicate sip.

He noted the flash of distaste in her eyes and the slight wrinkle of her nose. "You don't care for it."

"It's rather sweet."

Their plates were set before them, effectively interrupting their nascent dialogue.

Mrs. Langton leaned close again, tempting Dare with her orange-and-lily scent. "You could ask what she likes to read. That should launch a lively discussion."

Tempting? Dare thought of their brief encounter that afternoon when she'd mocked him, lowering her voice to match his and thrusting her shoulders back to puff up her chest. Unfortunately, the action didn't make her appear larger or more substantial like him. It had drawn his attention to her rather perfectly curved torso, most notably her full breasts. Perhaps it hadn't been unfortunate after all.

That she'd teased him had stuck with him ever since. No one mocked him. Ever. Not even at school, where everyone was mocked.

Yet, Mrs. Langton talked to him in ways no one did. She looked at him with open hostility and agitation, all while continuing to smile and cajole him —in the name of her charge. She was utterly beguiling.

If only Lady Marina possessed even a fraction of her companion's energy, Dare would have no problem offering for her. She did not, however. He watched her as she gingerly ate a green bean. Her features were blank, and he wondered if they were schooled that way or if she was just completely devoid of emotion or reaction.

"Does she ever smile?" he asked Mrs. Langton, shocking himself. He hadn't really meant to share the thought aloud. Since when did he care about smiling?

"Do you?" Mrs. Langton countered.

"Touché." He tamped back a smile.

"Perhaps you and Marina should find equal ground there. You ought to have realized by now that you've much in common."

He supposed they *were* similar in demeanor. Turning his head once more, he took in her dark hair and pale, slender neck. She was an attractive woman, but he wasn't moved by her. There was no…spark.

"Do I trouble you, Lady Marina?" he asked softly.

Her head turned so sharply, he jerked, which caused her to flinch in return. "No." She immediately returned her attention to her pheasant.

Dare took the unsubtle hint and attacked his plate in earnest, ignoring both women despite being incredibly aware of Mrs. Langton. It was silly, but there was a heat to her that surrounded him. He reached for his wine.

"You really should ask her about books," Mrs. Langton persisted.

Dare downed the contents of his glass. "If you're so intent on seeing us matched, perhaps you should speak with her about how to engage with a gentleman she wishes to snare in the parson's trap."

Standing abruptly, Dare earned the attention of everyone in the dining room as conversation evaporated into silence. "Please excuse me."

He left the dining room, knowing his departure would be the talk of the house party. Not that he cared. People often talked about him, and he didn't care. Mrs. Langton and their hostess had been doing it just that afternoon, in fact.

Dare found himself in the library, where he plucked a book from the shelf and tucked himself into an alcove to read. If it hadn't been dark, he would have gone outside for a walk. A book about the wilds of Ireland would have to suffice.

He lost himself in descriptions of lush green hills and bold, crashing waves. He'd no idea how much time had passed when he heard a laugh.

"Poor Lady Cosford," a feminine voice said. Two women came into the library. Dare recognized them, but couldn't have recalled their names on pain of death. One was married to a member of Parliament. Huxley? Halsey?

"Don't pity her. This house party will be discussed for some—" The woman's voice cut off, and two pairs of eyes fixed on him in his alcove.

Hell. He'd hoped to be invisible.

"Oh dear. We beg your pardon, Your Grace," Mrs. H said, her face pale and her dark eyes wide.

"Were you discussing me?" Dare asked with a suffering sigh as he closed the book on his finger.

"Yes," the other lady responded, which earned her a stifled gasp and a shocked glare from her friend. The woman shrugged in response to Mrs. H. "Whom else would we be talking about?"

Mrs. H exhaled. She turned her focus to Dare. "You did cause a stir when you left dinner so abruptly."

"I know." And he didn't care.

"Oh, to be a duke, and do precisely as one pleases," not-Mrs. H said wryly.

Juno's words from earlier in the day came back

to him. Perhaps he took for granted the fact that he could do as he chose and behave as he liked without consequence.

Not-Mrs. H cast him a cautious look, as if she expected him to react negatively to her comment. "I suppose I am allowed certain...foibles. Or at least forgiven for them."

Dare suspected Juno didn't forgive him for a thing. Had he done wrong? He hadn't been entirely...pleasant during his promenade with Lady Marina at the picnic.

"Are you disagreeable on purpose?" not-Mrs. H asked while Mrs. H once again shot her a look of shocked distress.

Dare liked not-Mrs. H in the way he liked Juno. Neither suffered his grouchy demeanor. Well, not *precisely* in the way he liked the goddess.

"Not entirely. I don't generally like people." He shrugged, his shoulders scraping the back of the chair, as if that sentiment were common.

Not-Mrs. H's light blue eyes gleamed. "How refreshing to hear honesty from someone of our station."

Our. Was she peerage, then? He probably ought to know her name, but he wasn't going to ask. It wasn't that he didn't have the nerve. He doubted he'd remember, so why bother?

"W-why don't you like people?" Mrs. H asked tentatively.

Dare wasn't sure how to answer that question or if he even could. So he chose to ignore it. "Shouldn't you ladies be in the drawing room?"

"There is no rule requiring it," not-Mrs. H said with a laugh. "We went for a walk." She lowered her voice, a twinkle in her eye. "So we could gossip."

"About me." They'd already said they were talking about him.

Not-Mrs. H grinned. "Of course!"

Mrs. H pursed her lips as another flicker of worry passed over her features. "Lady Wetherby was most upset."

"Indeed." Not-Mrs. H edged closer to his chair, her expression eager. "Does this mean you aren't going to offer for Lady Marina?"

While he appreciated the woman's forthrightness, that didn't mean he would contribute to her gossipmongering. "That's between us." He used an even haughtier tone than usual in case the woman decided to grow even bolder.

Thankfully, she did not. Exhaling with an air of disappointment, she pulled back to her position next to Mrs. H. "I had to ask."

"You really didn't." He actually gave her a half smile, shocking her, which made him inordinately pleased. He had the sense that little surprised not-Mrs. H. Perhaps he should go to the trouble of learning her name. Or pay attention to who her husband was in case he recognized the man, if he was even in attendance.

Mrs. H tittered softly, provoking her friend to look in her direction and then share in her laughter. "This is much better than a walk," Mrs. H said with a cautious glance toward Dare.

He was certain their exchange would be bandied about as soon as they returned to the drawing room, not that he cared one whit.

"What of the treasure hunt tomorrow?" not-Mrs H asked.

There was to be a bloody treasure hunt? He longed to remove himself, but he'd come all the way to this party and ought to participate. Even if it grated his every nerve. "What of it?"

"It sounds most diverting," Mrs. H said with a nod. "We'll be put into groups. I daresay you and Lady Marina will be together."

There was absolutely no question they would. He began to wonder if the entire purpose of this house party was to push him and Lady Marina together. Lady Wetherby wanted her daughter to snag a duke, and Juno was certainly doing her part, as was Lady Cosford. But if there wasn't so much as a hint of anything between them, what was Dare to do?

He should give her one more chance. He'd been distracted by Juno at dinner, which had been foolish. Juno wasn't a potential duchess—Lady Marina was. She deserved his full attention and his best behavior.

Standing, he strode to replace the book on the shelf. He turned back toward the two women and inclined his head. "I bid you good evening."

Tomorrow, he would participate in the tiresome treasure hunt and try doubly hard to engage with Lady Marina. Hopefully, she would do the same with him, for he couldn't make this match on his own.

Couldn't he, though? He'd long told his mother that he didn't need a wife he could love, just an exemplary duchess. Perhaps he should prepare a list of questions about running a household and performing the duties of a duchess and simply ask Lady Marina each of them. That would tell him definitively if they would suit.

He'd compose a list as soon as he arrived in his chamber. How orderly and efficient. Just the way he preferred things.

CHAPTER 5

The following afternoon, Dare fortified himself with a small glass of brandy before striding into the drawing room where everyone was gathered for the insipid treasure hunt. His gaze went directly to Juno and then to Lady Marina, who stood at her side, head bent with her gaze locked on the floor as usual. Her mother, Lady Wetherby, was also there, but her attention was *not* on the floor. Her prickly stare was trained on Dare as he entered. He nearly turned and left.

"Good afternoon, Duke," Lady Cosford greeted him with another of her endless smiles. "I hear you took a rather long ride this morning."

Were the stables reporting his every action now? "Yes," he said simply.

"I'm glad. Cosford says riding is your favorite pastime, and we're delighted you find our stables to your satisfaction."

This time, he merely grunted. Her smile didn't falter, not that he'd intended it to. He didn't try to be surly. He just was.

"If you'll excuse me, I need to explain how the

hunt will work." She took herself off to where her husband stood near the hearth.

Dare made his way to the trio of women he'd regarded when he came in. Since he would undoubtedly be grouped with at least one of them, he might as well put himself in their proximity. Plus, he could savor Juno's intoxicating scent.

Lady Cosford discussed the treasure hunt, but Dare paid no attention. Instead, he went over the list of questions he'd drafted the night before. Today he would decide if he and Lady Marina would suit.

"I find it somewhat improper that I'm not part of your group." Lady Wetherby's acerbic tone cut into Dare's thoughts.

"I'll chaperone," Juno said brightly, glancing toward Lady Marina and then Dare, who stood just behind her, but also somewhat close to Juno.

"Very well." The countess gave Juno a pointed look rife with expectation before taking herself off.

Juno pivoted to face him and Lady Marina. "I'm confident we can win."

Dare appreciated the ruthless glint in her eyes. "Are you competitive, Mrs. Langton?"

She lifted a shoulder. "When I want to be. And when it's important." Her gaze darted almost imperceptibly to Lady Marina.

He had the impression Lady Marina was important and that Juno wanted her to win—not the treasure hunt, but Dare. Surprisingly, he wanted to support Juno in her quest. He would give Lady Marina his best today. Whatever that was.

Lady Cosford approached them and handed a paper to Juno. "This is your list of ten items. Whichever team arrives back here first with all their objects will win."

"What is the prize?" Dare asked.

"The winners will get to choose the seating arrangement for one of the remaining dinners."

He opened his mouth to say that was a terrible prize, but then clamped it shut. His gaze drifted to Juno, who gave him a slight, perhaps approving nod.

Lady Cosford moved on as Juno studied their list. She spoke while her eyes scanned the parchment in her hands. "An orange. I know where we can get one of those quite easily. The orangery."

Dare had seen the orangery from the exterior on his walks, but hadn't yet visited. "Shall we start there?"

"Yes, let's." Juno looked to Lady Marina. "Would you like to look at the list?"

"I suppose I should." The young lady took the list between her gloved fingertips. "There's a book, and I know precisely where it is in the library. I can go and fetch it while you go to the orangery."

"No, you can't," Juno said rather hastily. She summoned one of her captivating smiles. "I believe it's against the rules."

Since when had her smiles gone from irritating to captivating?

"Is it?" Lady Marina didn't sound convinced.

"I take it you'd rather spend your afternoon in the library," he said, trying to sound…affable. How in the hell did one sound affable? Perhaps he ought to smile. The thought made him want to curse. He stretched his mouth but couldn't quite do it. His expression was probably the opposite of affable. He relaxed his features into their normal, un-smiling state.

Lady Marina's blue eyes flashed with surprise. "Yes. But we can do the treasure hunt," she added.

"We can always just pretend to do it," he said. "Perhaps we'll get stuck in the library."

She nearly smiled then, her face softening. She was quite pretty. He tried to imagine being married to her, and with that, the things they would do together once they were wed. Specifically, the things they would do in the bedroom. But a vision of Juno flooded his brain. He glanced toward her as heat suffused him.

That was *not* helpful to his cause.

Dare recalled his list of questions. Knowing that Lady Marina would while away hours in the library told him the answer to one: what she liked to do for amusement. "Do you ride?" he asked, ticking another off.

"A little. I'm not very good."

"Riding is overrated," Juno declared. "Let us make our way to the orangery." She gestured for them to precede her from the drawing room.

Dare hung slightly back, preferring to walk beside Juno so he could interrogate her about her silly statement. "Riding isn't overrated. Perhaps you've never properly learned."

Juno cast him a sour look, her lids low over her eyes. "Perhaps I simply enjoy other activities more."

"We should take a ride, and I'll show you how exhilarating it can be."

"By we, I hope you mean you and Lady Marina, with me as chaperone."

"Er, yes." That wasn't at all what he'd meant.

"Speaking of Lady Marina, perhaps you might wish to catch up with her. She is likely halfway to the orangery by now."

"Of course." Dare stalked from the drawing room, irritated that he'd allowed himself to be swayed from his goal. He would focus his entire attention on Lady Marina and not be distracted by her goddess of a companion. A goddess who didn't care for riding. That fact should have disappointed him. Instead, he hoped he had the chance to change her mind.

Lady Marina! his mind screamed.

Moving quickly, he fell into step beside her and slowed his pace. He returned to his list. "I sense you are like me in that social gatherings are not your...preferred activity." How else to put that? "Do you have any reticence about hosting a ball or a large dinner party?"

Lady Marina took a moment to answer, and Dare couldn't read her expression. "I assume you have a butler and housekeeper who would help with such matters? And a secretary too."

"I have all those people at my disposal, and they are most capable. However, a duchess must also be comfortable with such events."

"Yes, I understand. I'm sure I can be up to the task." She didn't sound sure.

Ah well, she was right. Others could do most of the work. She need only be charming and look beautiful. How shallow that sounded. Surely he wanted a bride who was more than that?

He glanced over his shoulder to see if Juno was following them. Perhaps she intended for them to be alone, despite the potential for scandal.

The goddess was there, trailing them at a discreet distance. Not entirely alone, then, but she was giving them space.

They reached the door that led to the covered walkway between the house and the orangery. He opened it for Lady Marina, who preceded him outside into the temperate autumn afternoon.

It was a short walk to the orangery, where he again held the door for Lady Marina. Inside, the temperature jumped several degrees. All around them sprouted vegetation, and the air was thick with the smell of dirt and life. He loved the scent of the outdoors, but this was different, perhaps because it was an artificial space. Things were brought here to grow in a controlled environment instead of allowed to flourish—or not—on their own.

Lady Marina was already making her way to the orange trees, which had been brought inside in their large pots. They sat at the opposite end of the building. He couldn't see any oranges from here and wondered if this would be a fruitless effort.

Fruitless.

"Are you *smiling?*"

He pivoted to see Juno standing just inside the door staring at him as if he possessed a second head. His pulse picked up speed, and his stomach knotted. The sensation was reminiscent of the time Cook had caught him pilfering a biscuit from the kitchen when he was six.

"No."

"Yes, you were." She narrowed her eyes at him. "Why wouldn't you want me to see you smiling?"

"I can't see any oranges." He started walking toward the trees, hoping she would drop the matter of whether he'd smiled or not. Yes, he'd bloody smiled.

She hurried beside him. "You are the strangest man."

He kept silent until they reached the other end of the building. "Find any?"

Lady Marina was on the other side of the grouping of trees. She poked her head around one. "Not yet. Oh, wait, there's one." She moved behind another tree, then reappeared with an orange in her palm. "What do I do with it?"

Juno held out a basket. "Just drop it in here."

Lady Marina rolled the orange into the basket.

"Now to the library." She turned and strode purposefully toward the door.

Dare frowned after her. "Is she in a hurry to reach the library or to get away from me?"

"Did something happen?" the goddess asked sharply.

"No. I just don't have the sense that she likes me."

"She doesn't know you."

"I am trying to engage her. There is just no..." He'd been about to say attraction, but decided that wouldn't be appropriate.

"No what?"

"No connection."

She flinched. "You need time for that to develop. Instant...connection is very rare."

"Are you speaking from experience, Mrs. Langton? Was there a Mr. Langton?"

"Yes, there was. However, my experience doesn't signify," she said imperiously, and damn if he didn't almost smile again. He liked provoking her, apparently. That was nearly as surprising as him smiling.

"Just give it some time," she repeated. "It's only been a few days."

"I don't think time is going to change this situation." There was no connection, no attraction, no anything drawing him to Lady Marina—or she to him—save the push of those who sought to match them together. The goddess in front of him, on the other hand, provoked an extreme attraction. But he couldn't say that.

Why couldn't he? Since when did he censor himself?

"The situation doesn't need to change," she said icily. "*You* do."

"Me?"

"You're obnoxious and rigid. I don't think you have it in you to do what's necessary to entice a woman to wed you."

"You don't think Lady Marina plays any role in this? She's perhaps less interested in this union than I am. At least I try to draw her into conversation. She behaves as if I'm anathema."

"So it's her fault that you're a complete boor?"

He winced, hating that his goddess thought so poorly of him.

She arched a brow at him and set a hand on her hip. "Perhaps you don't feel a connection with Marina because you're incapable of feeling that for anyone. Have you considered that?"

"I don't have to," he said softly. "I do feel a connection with someone. In fact, she drives me mad with her giddy smiles and forthright demeanor. I want to learn every single thing about her even though I shouldn't. More than anything, I want to kiss her and see if she'll taste as divine as I expect."

As he spoke, Juno's eyes went from narrowed to round. Her face paled shade by shade until she was the color of fine bone porcelain. "You can't mean...*me*?"

He moved toward her, his pulse thrumming as his body sang with want. "I can, and I do."

CHAPTER 6

*J*uno froze as the duke invaded the space directly in front of her—far too close for a gentleman to come. She ought to move the basket she held between them, but didn't. Because her heart was beating frantically, and her breath was coming faster and faster.

He wanted to kiss her. She hadn't considered that. Not because she didn't find him attractive. She just hadn't allowed herself to think of him in that way. But now that was *all* she could think of. His lips covering hers, his hands touching her—

She shook her head. "That would be bad."

He stopped moving, one dark brow shooting up. "Bad?"

"You need to court my charge—Lady Marina. You should make her your duchess."

"I've already explained that I doubt the match will be acceptable to either of us," he said patiently.

He seemed utterly at ease, while she worried about her ability to catch her breath. He was the most frustrating man!

The sound of the door opening and voices in conversation carried from the other end of the orangery. They both snapped their heads in that direction before looking at each other.

"I thought I saw another door in the corner," he said, moving swiftly past the orange trees.

She followed him, clutching the basket with both hands. Thankfully, there *was* a door, because the voices were moving closer.

He opened it, and unfortunately, it was only a cupboard for gardening implements. "Do we go inside or explain to whoever is coming why we're here and Lady Marina is not?"

Juno swore under her breath and hurriedly preceded him into the cupboard. He stepped in behind her and closed the door.

Darkness didn't descend, for there was a window high on the wall opposite the door. She held the basket in front of her, a sad shield between them. A shield? It was necessary, she reasoned. He'd said he wanted to kiss her. And she was not opposed. Indeed, the idea had rooted deep within her and taken hold.

She forced herself to listen to the conversation outside the closet. They were also looking for an orange. Hopefully, they would soon be on their way.

Juno let her gaze drift to his. His dark stare was fixed on her, coaxing the heat inside her to build. The small closet suddenly felt quite hot. She pressed one hand to her cheek and let the basket fall to her side, loose in her grip.

The voices outside began to diminish, as if they were returning to the house.

"I did try with Lady Marina," the duke said quietly. "Whatever you think of me, I did try. I realize I'm not the most charming of gentlemen." His mouth lifted in a small, self-deprecating smile, and it completely melted her.

He *was* an attractive man, but with a smile, he was absolutely captivating. She couldn't look away.

The smile began to fade. "What?"

"You did it again," she whispered. "Smiled. Why?"

"Because you're here."

"Oh bollocks." She dropped the basket and grasped the lapels of his coat, dragging him toward her. Not that he needed much encouragement.

His arms came around her, and he kissed her. It wasn't gentle or tentative, and it sure as hell wasn't rigid. His lips were soft but firm, commanding hers as he tucked her against him, chest to chest, heat finding heat.

He angled his head as his tongue drove into her mouth. She reveled in his passion even as she was shocked by it. She clasped at his neck and shoulders, kissing him back with urgency and fire.

The press of his body was a delicious friction, but she wanted more. Twitching her hips, she arched into him. He was *definitely* the rigid duke.

Oh God, what was she doing?

Juno tore herself away, breathing harshly as she fought to regain her senses. "I shouldn't have done that," she murmured.

He stared at her, his gaze dark and hungry. "I didn't mind. I told you I wanted to kiss you."

"That doesn't mean we should have." Juno never regretted such things. Her independence gave her the freedom to engage in liaisons with whomever she chose—and she was usually quite selective. The duke had taken her by surprise, however, and if she wasn't careful, he was going to sweep her away. Just as her husband had done.

She didn't want a husband. And she certainly didn't want one like Bernard.

Plucking up the basket, she hurried from the closet without a word.

He followed her. "To the library, then?"

Just continue on their quest as though nothing had happened? She stopped and looked back at him, but the response she'd planned evaporated somewhere between her brain and her mouth. The latter had gone quite dry as she regarded him. No, it was the way he was regarding her—as if he wanted to devour her whole. Need throbbed in her core.

What could they do? It was bad enough that Marina was likely in the library without them. Perhaps the others who'd just left the orangery were there too and were wondering why Juno's charge was alone.

She groaned. "You are a terrible influence. Have you no redeeming qualities?" Actually, he did. As it happened, he was a very, very good kisser. "Don't answer that," she said as much to herself as to him.

Swinging around, she stalked from the orangery and into the house. He kept up with her easily, but was kind enough to walk a bit behind her. At least she thought he was being kind. Perhaps she was giving him too much credit. He had kissed her, after all.

No, she'd kissed him. The man her charge was supposed to wed. Whose match would earn her a bounty.

As they reached the library, she fished the list of items from her pocket and quickly scanned them. Presumably, Marina had already found the book they needed, and they could move on to the next object—an acorn. There had to be an oak tree close to the house.

"She's not here," the duke said simply.

Juno looked up from the parchment and still

found his gaze unnerving. "What?" She glanced around the library and was dismayed to see they were indeed alone.

"She's not here," he repeated. "Do you suppose she continued on the hunt?"

"It's possible." Juno had showed her the list. "The next item is an acorn."

"There's a spectacular oak near the rose garden." He walked to the window and pointed. "There."

Juno joined him and looked outside. "She's not there either."

"May I see the list?" he asked politely.

She thrust the paper at him and craned her neck to see more of the exterior.

He handed the list back. "Perhaps she's in the music room. A piece of music is after the acorn."

"Do you think she grabbed the book?" Juno looked back at the paper and read the title aloud. "Where would we find this?"

"Over here, I think." He strode to a bookcase near the corner and perused the shelves. "Not here. She must already have found it."

Wouldn't she have come back toward the orangery, then? Or would she have continued on? Juno had a sinking suspicion Marina had abandoned the game entirely.

"Let's go to the music room," Juno said, turning toward the door without giving him a chance to deter her. Or kiss her again.

No, you kissed him.

"Did you just growl?" he asked from behind her.

"No," she lied.

"Here I thought I was the only one who did that."

"Are you smiling again?" she asked without turning. He'd sounded like he was smiling.

"Perhaps." Now he sounded like he was *grinning*.

Oh, this was a disaster.

They arrived at the music room, but Marina wasn't there either. But the piece of music they needed was.

It seemed likely that Juno's suspicion was correct. She exhaled. "I think Lady Marina may have quit the hunt. You'll need to continue on—or not—without us for now. I must go upstairs and see if she's retreated to our chamber." She set the list into the basket and handed him the lot.

"I'll keep on it. How will you find me?"

"I've memorized the list. Though, I doubt we've any chance of winning."

One of his impossibly dark, thick brows arched. "Planning the dinner seating was that important to you?"

She nearly giggled. "You've a sense of humor."

"It's rather dry. Some don't appreciate it."

Well, I do. She clamped her lips closed lest she say something she would regret.

Without a word, she swept from the music room and hastened to the chamber she shared with Marina. As expected, the young woman sat in a chair near the hearth, her head bent over a book.

"Is that the book for our list?" Juno asked brightly, hoping Marina had just been distracted.

Marina looked up, her cheeks pink. "Yes, actually. I wanted to read it."

"You're sure you didn't want to avoid continuing?"

The pink deepened. "You know me too well," she murmured. "I did try to wait for you in the library, but you took so long to come that I thought you and the duke perhaps went somewhere else. It seemed I should retreat, and yes, I wanted to." She looked down at the book in her lap.

"It's all right. We were caught in the orangery with other guests." And with kissing. Guilt tore through Juno.

Marina looked up at Juno, her eyes glistening with unshed tears. "I just don't like the duke. It's not his fault. He was trying to be pleasant even though he didn't want to be. It's obvious he doesn't like me either."

Juno's heart twisted as she sat down in the chair opposite Marina's. "Please don't feel badly about this. I can't agree that he doesn't like you. He was only trying to get to know you. He possesses a gruff nature. Just as yours is tentative. I think you would grow to like one other. Indeed, the duke surprised me with a sense of humor just a short while ago."

"I can't see any way that we would suit," Marina said with a surprising edge of steel. "I know it will disappoint Mama—and you."

"I could never be disappointed in you." Juno felt the sting of failure. Lady Wetherby was insistent that her daughter wed the duke. Would she try to force her into it if the duke decided to offer for her? Was the duke even considering it after kissing Juno in the orangery?

What, you think he'd consider marrying you? You don't even want to get married again.

No, she did not. The sooner she banished the unfortunate encounter in the orangery from her mind, the better. Even so, she knew this marriage wasn't going to happen—she'd known it before she'd kissed him.

The door slammed open, making both Juno and Marina jump. Lady Wetherby stood at the threshold, anger emanating from her person.

This was bad.

The countess moved inside and closed the door with more force than was necessary. Her gaze landed on Marina and then shifted to Juno, who stood on wobbly feet.

"Is something wrong?" Juno managed to ask, though the question was ridiculous since something was clearly *quite* wrong.

"The duke has just informed me that he will not be offering for Marina." She cast a livid stare at her daughter. "He said you do not suit."

Marina said nothing but dropped her gaze to her book. Juno could see the young woman's shoulders quaking.

"He also said you agreed," the countess said through clenched teeth. "Is that true?"

An unintelligible murmur slipped from Marina.

"What's that? Speak up, gel!"

"She said it is," Juno answered. "I was going to speak with you after the treasure hunt. They both did try, but I'm afraid they mutually agreed the match would not benefit either of them." The fib fell easily from her tongue as she sought to smooth this over as best she could.

"Not benefit them?" the countess shrieked. "Marrying a duke would be most beneficial to my daughter! She had to have done something to turn him away. But there's no help for it. This has been a complete failure." Lady Wetherby's irate glare landed on Juno. "*You* have been a complete failure. Your employment is terminated immediately."

"No, Mama!" Marina leapt to her feet, the book clutched to her chest.

The countess curled her lip. "And you have a book. You aren't supposed to have any books."

"It was part of the treasure hunt," Juno said, her own anger rising. "Marina has done nothing wrong. The duke is a surly, unpleasant gentleman. Marina has avoided a lifetime of distress."

Lady Wetherby sucked in a breath. "She would have been a duchess! That is worth at least a modicum of distress." She held her hand out. "Give me the book. We're leaving first thing in the morning. We'll dine in our rooms."

Marina handed her the book and sent her mother a mutinous glance.

"Ungrateful chit," Lady Wetherby muttered. "You're going to end up married to the rector if you can't manage to pull yourself together." She turned her attention to Juno. "You will not be returning home with us, of course. It is up to you to find your way wherever you wish to go. I'll have your things sent to your residence in Bath. I will not provide a reference. Indeed, if asked, I can't recommend you *at all*." She clucked her tongue. "So disappointing since you were highly recommended."

With a final glower at both of them, the countess spun on her heel and left.

"Oh, Juno, I am so sorry." Marina's voice caught, and she covered her face with her hands.

Juno put her arm around the younger woman. "Don't cry over me. I'll be fine. Truly." Hopefully, Lady Cosford wouldn't mind letting her borrow a coach to return to Bath. That was the least of her worries, however. Far more troubling was how Lady Wetherby's anger would affect Juno's future prospects.

Also vexing was how Lady Wetherby's anger would affect poor Marina. Juno wished she could take the young woman with her. She'd be better off. She could read to her heart's content, and no one would pester her to marry anyone.

"I'm sorry your mother doesn't understand

you," Juno said softly. "Look at the bright side. At least you don't have to marry someone you don't want to."

"For now," Marina said bitterly. "She'll find someone else who's possibly more loathsome."

"You didn't really find the duke loathsome, did you?" Juno was finding him quite the opposite. Not that it mattered. Tomorrow, she would leave the house party and hopefully find a new position. If she moved quickly, she could secure something before Lady Wetherby had a chance to impugn her character.

Marina hugged her tightly, surprising Juno. "I'm going to miss you terribly."

"You haven't seen the last of me," Juno said with a smile. "I'll find a way to help you—if you want it."

"You're so very kind." Marina stood back and wiped her hand over her eyes. "The kindest person I've ever known. And the bravest. I wish I could be like you. I'm going to try. Starting with telling my mother I refuse to have another Season—at least not this year. She should focus her attention on Rebecca." Marina's younger sister was seventeen and could perhaps make her debut.

"Perhaps I'll run away to Scotland or Oxford. Yes, Oxford, where I can disguise myself as a man and steal into lectures."

Juno laughed, feeling slightly better at having to leave her charge. She'd managed her mother this long and would be fine. Not that Juno had any choice in the matter.

Marina exhaled and clasped her hands together. "I'm feeling quite better about things. As you said, at least I don't have to marry the odious duke."

"I actually named him the rigid duke," Juno said wryly, provoking a rare giggle from Marina.

"That fits him perfectly."

Juno had thought so, but after their passionate encounter in the orangery, she wasn't so sure. Nor was she going to find out.

And that left her with a twinge of disappointment.

CHAPTER 7

*A*fter dining in her chamber—not with Marina, who'd had to dine with her mother in the countess's chamber—Juno slipped from her room in search of a glass of brandy or port or whatever she could find. She was pleased to see the upstairs sitting room had a bottle of madeira set out with several glasses. Juno poured a small amount and situated herself in a chair to ponder her next move.

Cecilia strolled by the open doorway, and Juno called to her. "Care to join me?"

"I would, thank you." Cecilia went to pour herself some madeira before taking a chair near Juno's. "You were missed at dinner, as were Lady Wetherby and Lady Marina."

"Does everyone know they're leaving?" Juno asked.

"Yes. And it is just them?" Cecilia asked. "That's what Lady Wetherby told the butler."

"That is correct. I am not leaving with them because I am no longer in Lady Wetherby's employ." Juno pursed her lips before sipping her wine.

Cecila's brow furrowed. "I am quite sorry to hear that. Their failure to suit wasn't your fault."

"I doubt you'd convince Lady Wetherby of that," Juno said wryly. "She let me go without a reference. I'm afraid I shall have to ask you for transport to Wolverhampton so I may catch a coach to Bath."

Waving her hand, Cecilia gave her a warm smile. "Nonsense, you must stay for the remainder of the party. Then I'll send you to Bath in one of our coaches."

"That's awfully kind of you, but I couldn't impose."

"It's no imposition. Furthermore, I'd be delighted to recommend you. As I said, none of this is your fault. Some people are not meant to be together."

"I suppose, but I still feel we failed in our endeavors." Juno frowned at her madeira before taking another sip.

"Perhaps we should have expected it," Cecilia lamented. "There just wasn't anything between them, not even a kernel of curiosity."

"Plenty of people wed without so much as spending any meaningful time together." Juno shook her head. "Which is terrible. I confess I am not disappointed for Marina. She didn't like him."

"Did she even give him a chance?" Cecilia blinked. "It doesn't matter now."

Juno grimaced. "I'm not entirely sure she did. However, the duke did seem to try, today at least." Until Juno had ruined it by kissing him. Had she provoked him to speak with Lady Wetherby? Had her impulsive behavior cost her this position? Of course it had. She was quite furious with herself.

"He must have come to the conclusion that it was a lost cause," Cecilia went on. "I understand he explicitly informed the countess that he wasn't going to offer for Lady Marina."

Flinching inwardly, Juno said, "Yes, that's precisely what he did."

"Perhaps Lady Marina is better off," Cecilia suggested. "The duke is so very rigid and aloof."

"I did have doubts as to whether she would have been happy," Juno admitted. "Indeed, I think I may pity the woman who becomes his duchess."

"He seemed more relaxed at dinner this evening."

Juno sat up with interest. "Did he?"

Cecilia nodded. "He actually spoke with those around him and remained engaged throughout the meal. It was a far cry from the night before, when he abruptly left."

Indeed. "How extraordinary."

"He didn't so much as flinch when Lady Bentham asked if he was going to leave too since his prospective bride is departing early."

Juno bit back a giggle, briefly pressing her hand to her lips. "My goodness, what did he say?"

"He responded with a succinct 'no.' I did wonder if his behavior tonight is further proof that the match would not have worked. Without the pressure of having to determine if he and Lady Marina would suit, he was able to be more of his true self."

Juno snorted. "Doubtful. He's far too guarded to allow that. I'm just so shocked that he plans to stay when he hates house parties. What could possibly keep him here?" She cocked her head. "Perhaps it's your stables. He does seem to enjoy his morning rides."

"You've come to know the duke rather well. Likely due to your efforts to match him with Lady Marina."

"Yes."

Or was it something else?

"I wish you would stay too," Cecilia said. "Why not enjoy the house party as a guest?"

"I'm not sure your other guests would appreciate that. I'm not—"

Cecilia held up her hand. "Don't say you aren't one of us. I know your grandfather was a baron. *Is* a baron. I do believe he's still breathing."

"You are frighteningly well informed," Juno said good-naturedly.

"My mother ensured I committed *DeBrett's* to memory. It's settled, then. You'll stay." Cecilia didn't ask and likely wouldn't accept Juno's refusal.

"I shouldn't."

"But you will because we are now dear friends, and I'll be bereft if you leave." She pouted for good measure, but ended up grinning instead.

The giggle finally escaped Juno before she could press her fingers to her lips. "Fine. I'll stay. But I wager the duke will end up leaving. Again, what possible reason could he have to stay?"

Cecilia shrugged. "As you said, perhaps he likes the stables. Whatever the reason, clearly something at Blickton has captured his attention."

∽

*D*are leaned against the wall just down from the room Juno shared with Lady Marina and crossed his arms. Perhaps he should stand here all night so that he could catch Juno in the morning before she left. He couldn't let her leave without seeing her again.

And what did he expect would happen?

His former potential bride, Lady Marina, could very well come out first, and then what would he say? *"Pardon me, but I must speak with your companion."*

He dropped his arms to his sides and squirmed, feeling awkward just at the thought. If it actually happened, he'd probably leap out of his skin.

Then what was he doing here?

He couldn't seem to make himself leave. He'd likely never see Juno again if he did.

Just what will *you do if you happen to see her?*

He had no bloody idea. Exhaling, he pushed away from the wall. But before he could turn and leave, he caught sight of her. She was coming right toward him.

Garbed in a simple but elegant gown of dark pink and pale green, with her blonde hair styled exquisitely atop her head, she looked like a sugary confection. Certainly good enough to eat.

She walked past her door, slowing as she neared him. "Good evening, Your Grace. Have you come to tell Lady Marina that you've changed your mind? That you're a blockhead?" She smiled sweetly—definitely good enough to eat, even when she was insulting him.

She wasn't wrong.

"I *am* a blockhead. However, I have not changed my mind about Lady Marina. I came to see you."

That silenced her for a moment. "Oh. Why?"

"I didn't want you to leave before I said goodbye."

"You're loitering outside my room to say goodbye?" She snorted, and he found the sound absurdly attractive. A lady had never done that in his presence. But she was no ordinary woman.

"Is that so strange?"

"For you? Yes."

"You think you know me so well."

"Don't you start with that half smile again." She took a step back. "You've said goodbye. Now you should go to bed."

How he wished that was an invitation. Bed sounded very inviting, especially if she were in it. "Actually, I didn't." He couldn't bring himself to do it. Saying goodbye would make it real. Final.

She exhaled and put a hand on her hip. "It doesn't matter, because I'm not leaving with Lady Wetherby and Lady Marina."

A giddy thrill tripped through him. "You're not?"

"My goodness, you actually look and sound quite relieved." She narrowed her eyes at him. "What's gotten into you? In fact, why aren't *you* leaving tomorrow?"

"I'd planned to be here for the duration of the party. I don't like to change plans."

She blinked at him. "Even if it means staying at a house party when you loathe house parties?"

"I don't loathe this one."

"Why?" She sounded incredibly skeptical.

"Because I met you. Now that I know you aren't leaving, I'm particularly keen to stay so that I may get to know you better."

She stared at him and repeated, "Why?"

"I should think it was obvious. We kissed earlier. It was quite nice." He scowled and shook his head. "It was bloody brilliant."

"How charming of you to curse in reference to my kissing ability," she murmured. "It was a horrendous mistake. Anyway, I'm leaving day after tomorrow. I wanted to be on my way tomorrow, but Cecilia convinced me to stay."

"And Lady Wetherby doesn't mind?"

She narrowed her eyes until they were almost slits. "Lady Wetherby dismissed me."

"Because I don't want to marry her daughter?" He swore, and his gaze flew to hers. "My apologies.

Sometimes I forget to keep such things in my head."

"It takes much more than that to offend my sensibilities."

Another point in her favor. Was there anything about her that wasn't wonderful? Even her smiling was growing on him. Though, she wasn't smiling now. "That Lady Wetherby let you go because of my actions says far more about her than it does you."

"If only everyone thought so," she murmured. "It doesn't matter. She was unhappy with how things turned out, and I am the scapegoat."

"Better she's unhappy now than her daughter is for a lifetime. Neither of us wanted to marry the other. Lady Marina never failed to look positively tortured whenever she was in my presence."

Juno shook her head. "You aren't as self-aware as you think. You looked much the same in her presence."

He exhaled. "In my defense, I look like that most of the time when I'm in the company of others, especially at an event like this."

"Is it really torture?"

"It's...uncomfortable." He shifted his weight, feeling a flash of that familiar discomfort just from discussing it. "I prefer solitude or smaller gatherings." He was more than comfortable at the moment in only her presence. "It's quite taxing to spend so much time with so many people."

"Is it?" She seemed to contemplate his revelations, which he never shared with anyone. "You've described Marina exactly. It's too bad neither of you could get past that, for you have much in common."

He arched a brow at her. "Are you still trying to play matchmaker?"

"No. I need to move on, and I am ready to do so. I will search for my next position and hopefully find more success than I did with Marina." She sounded disappointed.

"I'm sure you did your best. Our failure to match wasn't your fault."

"Perhaps. However, I'd hoped to effect more change in my charge than I did. She improved her skills while I was with her, but overall, she's no more ready to wed than she was when I started." She pursed her lips. "Lady Wetherby was right in that I didn't achieve what I was hired to do with Marina."

"Somehow, I doubt that's your fault either."

Amusement creased the fine lines at the outer edges of her eyes. "How can you possibly know?"

"From what I can tell, you're extremely capable, so much so that you're in high demand. Doubtless, you will find another position quickly." He hoped not too quickly. Perhaps she'd end up staying more than just tomorrow.

"I hope you're right. If Lady Wetherby's dissatisfaction spreads, my demand may plummet. I must get to bed. It will be an early morning seeing Marina off, and I'll need to get started on my correspondence. I will likely spend most of the day doing that."

She started to turn, and he felt a surge of longing. He nearly begged her not to go, but they couldn't continue to stand outside her chamber. "Surely it won't take so long. If the weather is fine, take a walk with me. We'll visit the oak that would have provided us with our winning acorn."

Her brow creased, as if she was confused. "Why are you suddenly charming? You are a most bizarre gentleman. The acorn would not have ensured our victory. We had several other items to obtain."

"I am confident we would have emerged triumphant."

"Because of the acorn."

"Why not?" He felt the side of his mouth tick up and noted her reaction.

Her beautiful green eyes narrowed once more. "Why are you behaving in this manner? Forgive me, but your current demeanor is not at all what you've presented the past few days."

"I like you. I have no discomfort when I am with you."

She froze for a second, then blinked. "Oh. Well, good night, then." She abruptly turned and went into her chamber.

He stared at the closed door for a moment, pleased with how the conversation had gone. Perhaps coming to this house party wouldn't be a complete waste of time after all.

CHAPTER 8

Satisfied with her progress, Juno shook her hand out after drafting four letters to people who'd inquired about her services in the time that she'd been working for Lady Wetherby. She'd ask Lord Cosford to post them and hope at least one would bear fruit.

She rose from the desk and glanced about the room, which was rather disheveled from Marina's departure and the fact that since Juno hadn't left it yet that day, no one had come to tidy it. She supposed she should give them that chance, meaning she should leave.

A look toward the window said it was a fine day indeed. Perfect for a walk with a rigid duke. A handsome and suddenly charming rigid duke.

I like you.

Those three simple words had stayed with her all night and were currently propelling her to accept his invitation. The memory of his lips on hers, of his tongue licking erotically into her mouth, of his hands clasping her body and leaving her aquiver, rushed over her. He'd invited her to walk, not to engage in a liaison.

Would she?

She was between positions, and she'd made a habit of taking a lover during those periods. None of them had been dukes, however, rigid or otherwise. In fact, none had been titled at all. Was his lofty station a deterrent? Certainly not. His disagreeability was.

Except he'd become far less brusque, at least with her. He'd been gruff with Marina, but then Marina hadn't been exactly pleasant to him. She also understood his behavior now, that he truly struggled around most people. Honestly, he and Marina really were so very much alike. Perhaps that was why they didn't suit.

Saying goodbye this morning had been difficult, but Marina had displayed a steel and determination that had alleviated Juno's fears. She suspected Lady Wetherby would be in for a shock if she pushed too hard. Perhaps Juno had been more effective than she'd originally thought.

A golden leaf floated past the window, and Juno decided to take advantage of the glorious day. Quickly changing into a smart, dark blue walking dress, she grabbed her gloves and a fetching widebrimmed hat, along with the post she intended to give to Lord Cosford, before dashing downstairs.

Finding the butler, Juno gave him the letters, asking him to deliver them to her host. Now, where would the duke be?

As she neared the drawing room, which seemed to be the headquarters of the house party, she heard voices. Walking inside, she was met almost immediately by Cecilia. "Oh, there you are, Juno. I was just going to send up for you. We've planned an impromptu walk to the village since the weather is so lovely."

Juno scanned the room and found the duke standing in the corner, wearing his usual scowl.

What had happened? Why had he reverted to his ill-natured self?

"We'll walk to the village and take refreshment at The Wayward Knight," Cecilia continued. "Then coaches will bring us back so that we have time to rest and change for dinner."

"That sounds splendid," Juno said, darting a look toward the currently *very* rigid duke. "Pardon me a moment." She went to where he stood in the corner. "You look as if someone has stolen your horse."

He blinked at her in surprise. "I can't possibly look that angry."

She laughed softly. "I don't know how angry that would make you, but you do appear quite disgruntled. What's happened to cause your wretched mood?"

"I don't want to walk to the village with everyone."

"But you invited me to walk today. In fact, that's why I came downstairs."

Another flash of surprise, but different from the previous—there was a spark in his gaze too. Anticipation, perhaps. "Is it?"

"Now I wonder if I should find someone else to walk with."

"No," he said quickly. "I just… This is not the walk I had planned."

She cocked her head to the side. "What *did* you have planned?"

"Just the two of us."

"I see." She thought of what he'd said the night before about not being able to tolerate so many people and about not liking to change plans. "What if we walk behind everyone else?"

He relaxed, his shoulders dipping. She could see some of the tension leave his frame.

"Why are you so very rigid?"

"I like routine. I like knowing what's expected."

"You don't like surprises, and this spontaneous activity has set you off-kilter."

Appreciation warmed his gaze. "You understand."

"I think I do."

A smile teased his lips, and she wished he would just outright grin. He was even more handsome when those flashes of humor lit his face. If he allowed it to take over, she suspected the effect would be devastating.

Cecilia came toward them. "Ready, then? We're going to leave in a few minutes. Unfortunately, Lord Cosford isn't able to join us due to an emergency with one of his horses."

The duke's brow furrowed. "I hope everything is all right. Does he need any help?"

"I'm sure all will be well. Thank you for your concern, Duke." She inclined her head toward him, then departed.

Juno was a bit surprised she hadn't lingered. She rather expected Cecilia would want to walk with her, which would ruin the duke's revised expectations. Perhaps she wouldn't. And if she did, well, Juno would deal with that problem when and if it arose.

She turned to him as the others began to leave the drawing room. "I suppose we should be on our way."

"I'm amazed you're able to perceive me so well."

She cast him a sly look as they waited for everyone to precede them from the room. "I'm not sure that's flattering."

"I only mean that you're so different from me. You aren't rigid—I believe that's the word you used —at all. You're cheerful and charming, obviously quite comfortable with any number of people around you. I wonder if you thrive on it."

"I do. Somewhat. I'm always keen for a reprieve." She sent a look toward the last of the guests leaving and whispered, "Especially with Society types."

He laughed. "Am I not a Society type?"

She stared at his face, shining with amusement. Absolutely devastating. "Oh, do that again."

"What?"

"Laugh. Promise me you'll do it again before the day is over."

"With you beside me, I'd say that's a great possibility. I don't recall the last time someone provoked me to laughter." He looked at her in bemusement. "That's what I mean—we're so very different. You are light, the very sun, while I am darkness. Not even the moon, for that can glow brightly. Rather a void."

She frowned at him. "You can't think that about yourself. You are certainly not a void." She grasped his forearm and gave him a squeeze. "See? You're flesh and bone, a man." Suddenly, she was thinking of him in the most primal way.

"We should go before we can't catch up." She spun on her heel and started from the drawing room.

He walked beside her once they left the room. "You didn't answer my question. Am I not a Society type?"

"Heavens, no. You're a duke, of course, but I gather you loathe Society. And you certainly don't behave like anyone I've met in Society."

"You've met a great many people like that?"

"My grandfather is a baron, so yes, I've met enough."

He looked genuinely surprised. "How on earth

does the granddaughter of a baron end up as a paid companion?"

"My dear duke, we're all just a decision away from a completely different life. Only think of your near engagement to Marina. If you'd decided to propose, everything would have changed for you already."

"This sounds like a story I'll need to hear on the way to the village. Will you tell me?"

"You'll have to tell a story of my choosing in return." Juno didn't yet know what she would ask, but she'd think of something.

They stepped outside into the sunlight, and Juno looked up at him. "Do we have an accord?"

"We do." He looked at her intently, his dark eyes seemingly trying to see every part of her. "Now tell me about the decision that changed your life."

⁓

*I*t wasn't what Dare had envisioned when he'd invited Juno to walk with him today. It was better. He hadn't anticipated the curl of joy threading through his chest or the absolute rightness of how it felt to be with her, as if there were nowhere else he was supposed to be.

They walked several paces behind the nearest trio of people. Everyone was somewhat spread out along the track, golden sunlight bathing them as trees painted in a riot of color lined the right side.

"Deciding to marry Bernard Langton changed my life," she said simply. Then she smiled and shook her head. "Actually, it wasn't the deciding part exactly. It was when I informed my parents that I wanted to marry the dashing schoolteacher I'd met at the local assembly. They were horrified."

He looked over at her, resplendent in her dark

blue walking gown trimmed with bright gold. "Because he was a schoolteacher?"

"Not *just* because of that, but yes, that was a factor. He was also boisterous and charming—excessively so is how my mother described him."

"He sounds like he was a good match for you. You're very charming."

"My mother would argue that was why I needed a husband who was more sedate."

"She thought you needed calming?" Dare wouldn't change a thing about her. *Now.* When he'd first met her—a scant few days ago—he'd thought she smiled too much, that she was too... energetic. That seemed ludicrous given how much her smiles and energy lit the world. *His* world.

Another laugh. "Why, yes, she did. More importantly, she wanted me to marry someone respectable. Bernard was loud and opinionated. People either adored him or reviled him. I fell into the former category, of course. He also tended to drink more than he ought." She winced, and he wondered how Langton had met his demise.

"What happened to him?"

"I'm not entirely sure. He didn't come home from the pub one night. The blacksmith found him at the bottom of a hill just outside town, facedown in a stream." She spoke matter-of-factly, as if she either no longer grieved him or hadn't grieved him at all. Except she'd said she adored him.

He studied her profile, noting the slight pucker of her brow. "Do you suspect something sinister?"

"Not really. It's likely he was intoxicated and suffered an unfortunate accident."

"Had you been married long?"

"Less than a year. As you can imagine, he left me in a bit of a state," she said wryly. "I couldn't go back to my family, not after they refused to even attend our wedding. I responded to an advertisement for a paid companion in Bath. While there, I helped my employer's wallflower granddaughter to secure a husband. Another woman offered to double my salary if I would come and help her daughter do the same."

"So you left your employer?"

She shook her head. "Lady Dunwoody gave me a chance when I most needed it. I stayed with her until she passed away about a year later."

"You're loyal."

"To a fault, some might say." She grinned at him. "I think it's important to stand by your principles and alongside the people you've pledged to help or who mean something to you."

He suspected her fierce loyalty stemmed from the fact that her family hadn't stood by her. A need to remain at her side, to show her that she was valued rose strong within him.

"What an admirable quality to possess," he said softly.

"I've told you about my life-changing decision. Now it's your turn to answer my question."

"I haven't made any life-changing decisions," he said.

"I didn't think you had. You wouldn't like your life changed. You didn't even like the parameters of today's walk changed." There was humor in her tone, and he couldn't help but feel a buoyancy that only she evoked.

"Is that why you didn't give Marina a chance? Marriage is a massive life change. Perhaps you're not ready for that."

He flinched inwardly. A direct hit. "I did try to give her a chance. She just wasn't what I'm looking for."

Juno tipped her head as they walked, one eye

assessing him. "Then here is my question. What are you looking for in a wife? What would motivate you to completely upend your life?"

When she put it like that, he wasn't sure he wanted to upend his life. But he must. "I am a duke, and I need a duchess. I came here because my mother insisted I would find her. I believe she worked with Lady Cosford to set up this entire house party for the purpose of matching me with Lady Marina. Everyone, it seems, believed we would suit perfectly."

"Except you didn't."

"No, we did not, and it wasn't for lack of trying. You either engage with someone or you don't. I realize many people wed without feeling a sense of connection or...rightness, but I am not one of them."

"This is also an admirable quality," she said solemnly. "Truly. I must apologize for haranguing you about not trying to make it work."

"As you said, on the surface, the match seemed ideal. However, appearances are not always what we think. Only consider you and Langton—you were deemed an unsatisfactory match by your family and yet you knew it was the right decision."

"I suppose you're right, but in the end, things didn't turn out well for me and him. Perhaps my parents weren't entirely wrong."

"You mustn't doubt yourself, especially about things that have already transpired. You can't change what happened. You can only determine how it affects you."

"My goodness, but you possess far more depth than I anticipated. And that was my mistake," she added with a soft smile. "You still haven't answered my question. What sort of woman will provoke you to wed?"

He thought for a moment before answering. "Someone who appreciates life—not the trifles of Society, but the simple joy of a walk on a beautiful autumn day. Someone with courage and strength, who doesn't need the title of duchess to feel accomplished." He hesitated before adding, "Someone who won't cower from me or find me too...rigid."

Her gaze met his with sympathy and a tinge of something else—regret, perhaps. "I hope I haven't insulted you. Sometimes I should really learn to hold my tongue."

"Not at all—on either count. Your forthrightness is another admirable trait." He realized everything he'd said described her perfectly. She radiated joy and strength. She was a woman who'd made the choices she wanted and made no apologies.

She also provoked him to smile and even laugh. To step outside his rigidity—to use her word—and to even find joy in spontaneity.

The silence stretched between them, punctuated by the nearby song of a bird. He hoped he hadn't made things awkward. He wasn't the most socially adept person. "Perhaps I ought to hire you to help me find a wife."

She sent him a sharp look, then laughed. "You're joking."

"Yes. I realize I don't do that very often."

"You're loosening up, then?" she asked.

"Apparently. I came on this walk when I didn't really want to, didn't I?"

She sent a gentle elbow into his arm. "Come now, did you really not want to come? I heard you take a walk every day. And a ride."

"I love being outside. Just not with a host of

others." He inclined his head toward everyone in front of them.

"Are there other people here?" she asked coyly. "I hadn't noticed."

In truth, he'd barely registered them either. He'd been too focused on her, too engrossed in their conversation. Her green eyes glittered in the afternoon sunlight, and he silently acknowledged that he'd never met a more beautiful woman—and not just on the outside.

The village came into view as they crested a small hill. He didn't want this surprisingly idyllic walk to end.

"I'm glad I decided to stay at the party," he said. "Are you?"

"I am."

And yet she would leave tomorrow. Unless he could persuade her to stay. For what reason? Because he couldn't bear for her to go.

"Will you change your mind about departing tomorrow? We could take another walk. Or better yet, ride with me in the morning. You said it was overrated, but I'd like to prove you wrong. I could also help you improve your chess game."

She slowed, almost to a stop. "My goodness, that would be quite a full itinerary, and I admit to being enticed. I should love to improve my chess game, and I'm just as eager to prove to you that riding *is* overrated. Still, I should probably go. I've posted letters today in the hope of securing my next position. I'll need to get home to Bath, where I can receive responses."

"What if I hire you?"

"To find you a wife?" She smiled softly. "I thought you were joking."

"I was, but now I'm not." He'd do anything to get her to stay.

"Thank you, but no. I have no expertise in that. I work with ladies, not gentlemen."

"Can't you see I'm in need of learning flexibility and charm? It can't be any harder than working with young ladies."

She laughed then and touched his hand. Though they wore gloves, the connection jolted him. He wanted to take her in his arms and rekindle the kiss they'd abandoned yesterday.

He glanced toward the people who were now rather far in front of them, for they had managed to stop walking. While the others weren't close, any one of them could look back and would see them embracing. If he kissed her. Which meant he couldn't. He let the anticipation and sexual tension curl inside him as she withdrew her hand.

She licked her lower lip, and he nearly groaned. "I don't think I can help you. Indeed, I believe you already possess the ability to relax and allow your humor and charm—yes, I think you possess charm—to come through. Just stop keeping everyone at arm's length. I understand it's difficult, but the more you allow yourself to be vulnerable, the more rewarding relationships will be."

Yes, he wanted exactly that. With her. He'd already shared more with her than he ever had with anyone. He liked how that felt. He didn't want to go back to locking everything up inside.

"We should keep moving," she said with a smile before hastening into a fast walk.

He wasn't going to let her avoid answering his question. "Even though you've refused my offer of employment, will you stay? At least one more day?"

She looked over at him, another smile—how had he ever disliked them—teasing her lips. "I'll consider it. Now don't pester me. I'd much rather hear about your favorite horse. I assume you have more than one."

Dare launched into a discussion of his favorite horses and did his best to enjoy the present. He'd savor every moment he had with her.

CHAPTER 9

By the time they reached The Wayward Knight, Juno wasn't sure she knew the duke at all. She also wished she wasn't still calling him "the duke" in her head. She knew his name. He was Alexander Brett, Duke of Warrington. Did his family, which seemed to just be his mother, call him Alexander? Alex? Probably not. Presumably, he had a courtesy title, not that she recalled what it was. His mother likely called him that.

Juno noted that Cecilia hadn't slowed along the track even once for Juno and the duke to catch up. She had, however, cast a few glances backward, which told Juno that her hostess was aware they'd been lagging behind. Had others noticed she and the duke walking together?

Not wishing to spark any gossip or speculation, Juno made a point of leaving his company when they reached the inn. She made her way to the refreshment table to fetch a tankard of ale and moved to the edge of the private dining room allotted for their party.

As soon as Juno sipped her ale, another woman from the house party approached her. Lady Gilpin was perhaps forty with dark auburn hair and a warm disposition. She was a close friend of Cecilia's. "Mrs. Langton, did you enjoy the promenade?"

"I did, thank you. What a splendid day."

"Indeed. I pray you won't find me intrusive, but I've heard you're no longer employed by Lady Wetherby. Dare I hope you're looking for a new position?"

"I am, actually." Juno assumed Cecilia had told her. "Seeking a new position, that is." She refrained from mentioning Lady Wetherby or Marina at all. It was better that way.

Lady Gilpin's eyes lit. "How fortunate for me—and my daughter. She will be embarking on her first Season in the spring, and I would dearly love for you to prepare her."

"Tell me about her," Juno said with a smile.

"She's quite shy. She can never seem to find the right words when in social situations. It's as if her tongue is twisted in knots."

"I see. Well, that is something we can work on. How are her other skills?"

"Good, I think. Though, she could use a bit of help with comportment. If there's something to be spilled or an item of clothing to be torn, Dorothy will be the one to suffer it. I suppose she's clumsy." Lady Gilpin flashed a worried smile.

"I've helped other young ladies who are very similar to how you describe your Dorothy. I'm confident we can have her ready to conquer London next spring." Did that mean Juno would accept Lady Gilpin's offer? Companion to the daughter of a baronet wasn't the most illustrious position, but it was right in front of her. What if no one else responded to her inquiries because Lady Wetherby made quick work of denigrating her?

Better she secure a position now before she wasn't able to.

"Does that mean you'll come?" Lady Gilpin looked so happy that Juno couldn't possibly decline now. "Your reputation is exemplary. Indeed, I considered writing to you a few months ago, but my mother assured me you would be too busy to help someone such as my Dorothy."

Juno winced inwardly. The inquiries she'd sent were to a viscountess, two countesses, and a marchioness. If given the choice, would she have selected Dorothy?

It didn't matter, and she wouldn't feel bad for working to place herself in the highest echelons of Society. She was a woman alone in the world, and she'd been fortunate to build an independent livelihood. She'd be a fool not to take the best-paying, most distinguished position she could find. Just as she'd be a fool now to decline a job that was hers for the taking.

"I'd be delighted to help Dorothy," Juno said. "I don't ever commit to a specific time period, however. It may be that we complete our work together before the Season begins. I'll be able to give you a better assessment after I spend time with her. Is that acceptable to you?"

"Oh yes. Thank you so much." The woman's relief was palpable, and Juno was doubly glad she'd agreed. "I can barely contain my excitement. When can you start?"

"I need to return home to Bath first, but I can come to you a week after the house party ends. Will that give you time to recover?"

"That would be just lovely. Dorothy will be so pleased to have help. She can be so nervous."

Juno looked forward to helping her. She sounded a far sight easier than Marina had been.

That thought made Juno feel bad. She'd come to care for Marina a great deal, but she was rather difficult. She was the only young woman Juno had tried to help who hadn't really wanted assistance. Indeed, she would rather have been left alone.

They chatted a few more minutes before Lady Gilpin excused herself. Juno felt her own sense of relief at having secured a new position before Lady Wetherby could malign her. And now she had a bit of time before she had to start.

Her gaze strayed to the duke. He stood across the room with a pair of gentlemen, but he seemed rather disengaged. He was staring at her. When her eyes met his, he lifted his tankard in a silent toast.

An unexpected flash of heat swept through her. Unexpected? It shouldn't have been. Not after yesterday's kiss or the way her entire body had tingled when she'd touched him during the walk to the village.

The idea of spending a few days tucked away with the duke was incredibly alluring. And she was nearly certain he'd be interested in a liaison. Weren't house parties perfectly suited to such endeavors?

No, she couldn't risk her livelihood in that way. If Lady Gilpin were to catch wind of any impropriety on Juno's part, she wouldn't allow someone with such a base character to supervise her daughter. Juno would need to be on her best behavior until she left for Bath.

Cecilia approached her. "What did Lady Gilpin want?"

"To offer me a position helping her daughter. I assumed you'd told her I was looking for a new arrangement."

"I did, in fact. I've known Penelope for years. Are you going to help Dorothy? She's such a lovely girl but a rather awkward bundle of nerves." Cecilia smiled faintly.

"Yes, I've agreed to help. Thank you for mentioning me."

"It was my pleasure. I also came to tell you that you'll be riding back to the house with the duke and me."

At first, Juno had thought she was going to say only the duke. Because she hoped that would be the case? She couldn't deny there were far worse things than sharing a coach alone with the duke.

"I'd hoped to ride back with Sir Edmund and Lady Gilpin," Juno said. "So we could discuss Dorothy."

"Oh dear, I think they've probably already left. They were in the first coach. Anyway, you're the only person I trusted to ride with the duke. He frightens everyone else." Cecilia laughed.

Juno wasn't amused. Now that she knew the duke better, she understood his eccentricities. He wasn't at all scary. "Is that true?"

Sobering, Cecilia pursed her lips briefly. "Not exactly, no. He doesn't frighten most of the gentlemen, but they are all riding with their wives." Right, and there were no other single gentlemen. By Cecilia's design.

Cecilia turned toward the door. "I'd best oversee the departures. The conveyances are already outside."

Juno finished her ale and set the empty tankard down on a table. As she started toward the door, she noted that most people had already left. Except the duke. He was waiting for her just inside the threshold.

"I understand we're to ride back together," he said. His voice was always so deep and tinged with that gruff growl that she liked more than she realized.

"With Cecilia," she clarified, lest he think it was to be just the two of them. Would he have looked forward to that?

"Yes." There was a darkness to the word, as if he were disappointed that they wouldn't be alone. A delighted thrill shot through her.

They moved into the main room and then outside into the yard, where the last group was climbing into a barouche. That left a rather small conveyance for the three of them who remained.

Except a gig pulled into the yard, and it was driven by Lord Cosford. Grinning, he waved at his wife. "I'm here, my darling!"

"Oh!" Cecilia put her hand to her chest, then smiled broadly. "What a wonderful surprise."

"I couldn't let the entire outing go by without an appearance," Cosford said. He looked toward the duke and Juno. "You don't mind if I steal the countess away, do you?"

Cecilia was already walking toward the gig as he jumped down to help her inside.

What could Juno say? She glanced sideways at the duke, who gave her an infinitesimal shrug. Furthermore, did she even want to say anything? Now she would be alone with the duke.

Her suspicions that Cecilia was orchestrating opportunities for them to be alone crystallized into certainty.

"See you back at the house!" Cecilia waved as her husband drove from the yard.

"I suppose that means we'll have the coach to ourselves," the duke noted. He offered her his arm and escorted her to the conveyance where the coachman waited.

The duke helped her inside and climbed in after

her. The space in the coach seemed smaller than normal. And dim. *Intimate.* The sun was low in the sky. Not quite dusk, though it would be soon. There was a lantern, but it hadn't been lit. Presumably, they would arrive at the house before it was dark, so lighting it hadn't seemed necessary.

Or perhaps Cecilia was trying to set a mood. Had she transferred her matchmaking to Juno now that Marina was gone? Juno didn't need a match. She was quite capable of remaining on her own and happy to do so.

"I do think Cecilia planned this," Juno murmured as the coach began to move.

"Do you?" The duke's thigh wasn't touching hers, but if she moved slightly, it would be.

Juno shook her head. "Who knows. We'll be back at the house shortly."

"Pity that."

She jerked her head toward his. "Why?"

"Because there are at least a dozen things that have come to mind—and more by the moment—that I should like to do to you in a private setting such as this." He angled himself toward her. "The question is, will you allow me to?"

The world fell away so that it was just Juno, the duke, and the crashing beat of her heart. Oh hell, she couldn't keep thinking of him as "the duke." "What do people call you?" she asked throatily. Swallowing, she added, "People you like, I mean."

He grinned, and she nearly threw herself at him.

"Dare. It's short for the courtesy title I held before I inherited—I was Marquess of Daresbury."

"Dare." That was possibly the best and worst name she'd ever heard. She didn't want to be dared by him, and yet she was. Thoroughly and devilishly tempted.

His eyes slitted, and desire pooled in her core. "No one has ever said my name like that." He was so close, she was enveloped in his rich, masculine scent. His raspy breathing filled the coach, matched only by her own short, shallow breaths.

"It's a very short trip to the house." She curled her hands around his neck. "We'd best hurry."

~

*D*are encircled his arms around her waist and hauled her against him. He slanted his mouth over hers and lost himself in the intoxicating rapture of her embrace.

This was spontaneous and reckless—completely at odds with who he was. He didn't care. He couldn't help himself. Everything he expected, everything he knew, disappeared next to Juno. She was a light, a temptation, an absolute craving.

He kissed her deeply, pouring all his pent-up tension and emotion into this moment. She clutched him tightly, her tongue sliding against his with a fervor that matched his. That she wanted this as much as he did made his spirit soar. This was bliss. He'd never felt it before.

Their positioning on the seat was awkward, made doubly so when they hit a bump on the road, and she nearly fell. Dare clasped her more tightly. She slid her leg over his lap and straddled him, rising over him.

"Better?" she murmured between kisses.

He growled into her mouth and kissed her again, one hand holding her nape and the other gripping her hip. Yes, better, but not good enough. He wanted her against him. Completely.

No, he wanted to be inside her. But there wasn't time for that. They'd arrive at the house before either of them would finish. Or not. The level of his desire was a heretofore unknown height.

He tugged gently on her neck as he kissed down her jaw, his lips and tongue finding their way to the hollow of her throat. How he wished she was wearing something that didn't button up so high.

She began to adjust her skirts, which were bunched between them, pulling at the yards of fabric until there was less separating them—just his clothing. Then she sank down on him, her sex a delicious heat against his stiff cock.

Arching up, Dare pressed against her, simulating intercourse. How desperately he wanted to sheath himself inside her. She rose up, then ground down again. He moved with her and brought her mouth back to his, holding tightly as he tried to maintain some semblance of control.

She whimpered into his mouth, and he slipped his hand from her hip, finding the end of her skirts and the start of her flesh. Grazing his fingers along her thigh, he sought her sweet core. As she lifted up once more, he touched her there, teasing her clitoris and drawing a low moan from her throat.

"Let me," he whispered as he worked his fingers over her flesh.

"Yes," she breathed. Then louder, "*Yes.*"

He stroked her into a frenzy, her body moving against his hand. "Come for me, Juno."

"I need you inside me. Please."

Happy to oblige, he thrust his finger into her and pumped. She cast her head back and moaned. He felt her muscles tighten around him just before she cried out.

"Shhh," he urged, claiming her mouth again as she rode her orgasm.

She barely stilled, her ragged breaths filling the coach, when they stopped in front of the house.

"We're here." He gently pulled his hand from beneath her skirts.

She looked down at him, her eyes shining with satisfaction. "Thank you. I'm sorry you didn't get to…"

"Next time." He held her gaze and deliberately put his finger in his mouth, sucking the taste of her from his skin.

Her eyes narrowed with renewed desire as she slid onto the seat beside him and rearranged her skirts. Just in time too, for the door opened.

Dare climbed out, then helped her to the ground. He offered his arm, and they started toward the house.

"There shouldn't be a next time," she said, keeping her voice low. "I've just accepted a position from Lady Gilpin. I'm afraid I must be on my best behavior while I'm here."

"I'm sure we can be discreet. Ask anyone who's conducted a liaison during a house party. It happens all the time."

"That may be, but I can't risk my livelihood. I do hope you understand."

He couldn't let that be the end of it. He stopped before they reached the door, which was being held open by a footman. "Then let's go somewhere else."

She was a step in front of him and looked back. Her eyes glinted with amusement. "Where?"'

"Anywhere. So long as you're there."

Lady Gilpin stepped from the house. "Oh! My coach is already gone. I'm afraid I left my hat inside. I had to take it off after one of the pins came loose. Ah well, I'll have a footman fetch it." She smiled at Juno. "Coming in?"

"Yes." Juno gave Dare a rather enigmatic stare as she let go of his arm. Then she disappeared into the house with her new employer.

Dare frowned. That wouldn't be the end of it. Juno had opened something inside him, and he'd be damned if he'd let it slam closed.

CHAPTER 10

*B*y the time the final course was removed from the table, Juno realized her cheeks hurt from smiling. That was remarkable since she was a generally pleasant person, most often with a smile on her face. This was different, however. Tonight, she'd been singularly engaged with the man beside her. The man she'd once called the rigid duke, which seemed asinine now.

Not that *he'd* spent the entire evening smiling. He was still far more reserved than her, especially in the company of others. She noticed he was distinctly different, more at ease, when it was just the two of them.

Thinking of that brought to mind their short carriage ride back to the house that afternoon. It was no wonder she'd spent the evening in a state of elation.

Now it was time to remove to the drawing room with the other ladies, and Juno found she didn't want to leave. "Thank you for a delightful dinner," she murmured to Dare.

His eyes met hers with a smoldering heat, and she had to clench her thighs together against a wave of arousal. "The pleasure was entirely mine."

"Not entirely. Don't make me argue with you." She winked at him before departing the dining room.

As she entered the drawing room, she looked for Cecilia. Her new friend owed her an explanation.

Unfortunately, Juno had to patiently wait to draw their hostess away from Lady Bentham and Mrs. Hadley, two ladies who liked to talk incessantly. At last, she had Cecilia alone. Then a footman offered them glasses of madeira.

"Why thank you, Vincent," Cecilia said, taking one of the wineglasses.

Juno also took one and swallowed a sip as the footman moved on. She fixed an expectant stare on Cecilia. "Are you playing matchmaker with me and the duke?"

Surprise rippled across her features. "Of course not. Why would I do that?"

"I can't think of a single reason, particularly since you also recommended me to Lady Gilpin. However, I can't discount the ways in which I've been alone with the duke today."

"Because of the ride back in the coach?" Cecilia waved her hand. "I do apologize for abandoning you to travel with my husband."

"You also didn't spend any of the promenade with me, despite looking back to check on my progress." Juno narrowed her eyes. "You weren't checking my progress, though, were you? You were trying to see if I was still with Dare."

Cecilia's lashes fluttered. "'Dare?'"

A low sound vibrated in Juno's throat.

"Goodness, you sounded like him just then."

"I did not." Perhaps a little.

"Why are you calling him Dare?" Cecilia asked coyly.

Juno rolled her eyes. "Because I grew tired of calling him the rigid duke."

Cecilia's eyes rounded. "Did you call him that to his face?"

Ignoring the question, Juno took another sip of wine. "You also sat me next to him at dinner again when there was no reason to. Do you deny that you're playing matchmaker?"

Lifting a shoulder, Cecilia also drank. "Do you deny that you and he are attracted to each other?"

Was it obvious? Juno tamped down a surge of apprehension. "That doesn't signify."

"Doesn't it?" A glint of triumph lit Cecilia's eyes.

"You can't think he'd marry me. I don't even want to get married."

Cecilia looked down at her wine. "I'm sorry. I should have spoken to you first. It's only that, well, you seem to share the connection that he and Lady Marina lacked. Call me a romantic, but I believe in love." Her gaze drifted in the direction of the dining room, and Juno thought she must be thinking of her husband.

"I used to," Juno said quietly. "I think perhaps I stopped—at least for me—when my husband... Well, when he turned out to be not quite what I'd hoped." His penchant for drink and general lack of focus on her and their marriage had become troublesome before his death. She'd hoped they would get back to the bliss of their courtship, but then he'd tumbled down that hill.

"That sounds like quite a tale. If you believed in love once, you will again," Cecilia said with a smile. "You just need to meet the right person. Perhaps you already have."

"The duke?" Juno scoffed. "I am not in love with him." She was something, though. He wasn't at all the type of man she would have expected to provoke romantic thoughts. Yet she'd thought of him far too much since kissing him. Thoughts that had only multiplied—and intensified—since their ride together in the coach earlier.

"I just hope you aren't closed to the idea," Cecilia said warmly. "It would be a shame to miss out on something special, even if it isn't forever."

Of course it wouldn't be forever. He needed a duchess, and that could never be her. As tempted as she was by him, she needed to keep her eye on the future. That future contained Lady Gilpin's daughter.

To that end, Juno ought to go and speak with her. But the gentlemen started to filter into the drawing room, and Juno held her breath waiting for Dare to appear.

He filled the doorway, commanding her complete attention—from the thick, dark hair atop his head that she hadn't yet gotten to run her fingers through to the delectable athleticism of his body, obvious when he walked, but even more so when he held her in his arms. Heat suffused her, and she wondered how she would stay away from him for the duration of her stay.

No, she wondered *why*.

≈

*D*are's gaze found Juno perched on a chair, her attention focused completely on him. His body instantly reacted, his pulse picking up speed and his cock twitching. He'd desperately wanted to frig himself after their encounter in the coach, but there hadn't been much time before dinner. Plus, he was rather enjoying the sensation of being wholly on edge. Dinner had been a delicious torment. He only hoped there would be sweet relief later—not with his hand, but in Juno's arms.

Before he could make his way to her, he was intercepted just inside the doorway by the ladies from the library the other night. He'd since determined that Mrs. H was Mrs. Hadley; however, he still couldn't recall the other woman's name.

"Good evening, Duke," not-Mrs. Hadley said. Since she was referring to him in that manner, he could confirm at last that she was peerage. Unfortunately, that didn't help him recall her name. He really ought to have paid more attention during dinner. Not that he could have dragged his focus from Juno. "You seem in lively spirits despite the departure of Lady Marina this morning. Whatever happened?"

Both ladies looked at him with candid anticipation. Normally, their nosiness would annoy him. However, it seemed he was currently impervious to irritation.

That didn't mean he would allow their intrusiveness to pass. "You seem quite excited to gather the details. I'd rather not provide you with gossip."

"Pshaw," not-Mrs. Hadley, who was the bolder of the pair, expelled with a wave of her fingers. "You can either provide the truth, or people will come up with a story they like and that will become the truth."

He growled in response, but in the end, he didn't care. "I did not have romantic feelings for Lady Marina, nor did she have them for me."

Mrs. Hadley blinked up at him. "That's all? You simply decided not to wed?"

It hadn't been that explicit, of course. Perhaps he should have made sure. No, he was sure. She hadn't wanted him any more than he'd wanted her. "You see, it's not very interesting."

Not-Mrs. Hadley pursed her lips. "It is, though, because you were both allowed to make that choice. I married Bentham because my father decreed it."

Lady Bentham!

Mrs. Hadley nodded in agreement. "I did the same. My father-in-law and my father came to the arrangement a year before I even met my husband. How nice it must be to be able to choose for yourself."

Dare felt a pang of pity for them. Along with that came a wave of awkwardness. He didn't know what to say. He tried, "I'm sorry you're unhappy."

"We never said we weren't happy," Lady Bentham said with a chuckle. "I've done quite well with Bentham. Better than some." She arched a brow toward Mrs. Hadley, who again nodded toward her friend.

"Oh yes," Mrs. Hadley said earnestly. "We've both been fortunate."

"Well, you perhaps more than me, but I am a viscountess, so there's that."

The ladies laughed together, and Dare's awkwardness increased. He wanted to get to Juno.

Lady Bentham sobered as she pinned Dare with a serious stare. "You were wise to wait for someone for whom you will have romantic feelings. I do care for Bentham, but it's not a passionate love affair, which my dear friend enjoys." She cast a slightly envious glance toward Mrs. Hadley. "I am most grateful for my children, however. Bentham will always have a place in my heart for them, if nothing else."

"I must disagree," Mrs. Hadley said, surprising Dare. "I don't think His Grace needs to wait for romance. I didn't have that when I wed Hadley. I liked him when we met. I found him dignified and charming. It was a good basis for marriage." She looked to Dare. "I would encourage you to find a lady you like and respect. Passion may very well come later as it did for me."

"You think I should have wed Lady Marina," he suggested.

Mrs. Hadley arched a shoulder. "Not necessarily. But love may have come. You'll never know now, of course."

That stung. Not because he thought he'd missed out on some grand love with Lady Marina, but because he could very well miss that with someone else. He flicked a glance toward Juno. Rather, where she'd been and was no longer. He found her seated beside Lady Gilpin on a settee near the center of the large room. They were likely discussing her forthcoming employment.

Dare didn't want to have any regrets. He looked back to Lady Bentham and Mrs. Hadley. "Would you marry your husbands again, then?"

"Absolutely," they both said almost in unison.

"Excuse me," he said, finished with the conversation. He wanted to go to Juno, but she looked rather engaged with Lady Gilpin. Furthermore, he didn't want to raise any suspicions from the two busybodies. He ought to feel bad thinking of them that way, but they'd likely agree. They made no secret of trying to ferret out information wherever they could.

Fetching a glass of madeira from a footman, Dare went to brood in the corner. Normally, he would just have retired, but he was far too anxious to do that. Anxious? More like stretched taut with lust and hope.

Hope?

Because the future—even later tonight—was completely uncertain. And for the first time, he wanted something for that future. For tonight and perhaps even all the nights after.

Was he considering something...permanent with Juno? He certainly liked and respected her, as the ladies had advised he should do. Hell, what would his mother say if he came home with the intention to marry a paid companion—who was also the granddaughter of a baron? Surely the latter would count for something.

Scowling, he brought the wineglass to his lips and drained half of it. When had he ever cared what people said? Yes, that included his own mother. Not that her opinion didn't matter. But in this instance, perhaps more than any other, the only one that mattered was his. And Juno's.

He watched, patiently despite the roil of emotions and sensations inside him, as she conversed with Lady Gilpin.

"Did you enjoy the promenade to the village today, Duke?"

Dare dragged himself to the present and glanced toward the new arrival. Lady Cosford with one of her overly sweet smiles.

"Yes." He didn't bother keeping the growl from his answer.

She frowned briefly. "I beg your pardon for my frankness, but has something happened? You were so pleasant at dinner. I thought perhaps you'd finally settled in and decided house parties aren't so loathsome after all."

They weren't, but that was entirely due to Juno. That he couldn't be with her right now, that he had to allow her to talk with her new employer, drove him mad. This was a new experience. He typically did what he pleased. He'd never before had to consider someone else and whether his behavior would affect them.

He was a rather selfish prick.

"I can't help but notice your attention toward Mrs. Langton," Lady Cosford said quietly, leaning toward him. "I'm sorry you didn't match with Lady Marina, but perhaps all is not lost."

Slowly, he tilted his head toward hers. "What are you saying?" Did she know something he didn't?

"It seems to me that both you and Mrs. Langton enjoy each other's company. I would hate for the party to end without either of you determining how much."

Her vagueness was also going to drive him mad. "If you have something specific to say, I wish you would do so, Lady Cosford. I am not a man who appreciates innuendo or subtlety."

She stifled a laugh. "Just so. Juno likes you. She's attracted to you. She's also concerned about jeopardizing her employment with Lady Gilpin. So you must be discreet."

"Has Juno indicated she wants…" He didn't know how to finish that. Had she told Lady Cosford about what had happened in the coach? He couldn't see her doing that even if the two had become friends, and it seemed they had.

"She's indicated nothing specific. I'm only trying to be a good friend. You know where her room is located?"

"Yes." He swallowed, his body already roaring into full arousal.

"Then you'll know it's precariously close to Lady Gilpin's. You'll need to find another way inside."

"Are you certain she wants me to come?"

"No, but if she doesn't, she won't be shy about asking you to leave. And you will." She narrowed her eyes at him. "You will, won't you?"

"Of course. I'm not a scoundrel." Excitement thrummed within him. "Are you going to tell me how to gain access?"

"I am, but so help me, if you treat her poorly, there will be nowhere you can hide." She gave him a blistering glower.

"I may be disagreeable, but I am honorable and trustworthy. You have my word that no harm will come to Mrs. Langton. Indeed, I would put myself in the way of that ever happening. With my dying breath." The ferocity of his pledge surprised him. He meant every word.

Admiration sparked in her gaze. "Excellent. I believed you to be just that type of gentleman. Now, listen to me carefully."

She explained in exacting detail how he could access the servants' stairs and find his way to the dressing chamber that adjoined Juno's room. The idea of seeing Juno filled him with a thrilling anticipation.

What if she didn't want him to come?

Then he'd leave. Utterly dejected. But he had to try. Anything else would mean regret, and he'd already decided he wouldn't suffer that. Not with Juno. Not with the only woman who'd ever made him feel like a whole person.

He could hardly wait.

CHAPTER 11

*B*y the time Juno had finished speaking with Lady Gilpin, Dare had left the drawing room. Disappointment had dimmed her mood and stayed with her, even now, two hours later.

After speaking with Lady Gilpin, Juno had decided to leave for Bath tomorrow. The house party lasted three more days, but Juno wanted to get home and prepare for her new position.

Normally, she'd be filled with a joyful anticipation at the prospect of working with a new young lady. This time, however, she felt a slight unease, as if she was forgetting something. Not forgetting —ignoring.

She was apparently doing her damnedest to pretend Dare didn't exist. Or that the smoldering attraction between them had petered out. Only it hadn't. Not for her anyway. She had no idea if he felt the same, especially since he'd left the drawing room without a word.

Rising from her dressing table, she flipped her long braid over her shoulder as she made her way to the bed, which a maid had turned down invitingly. Juno stared at the empty space and wished she wouldn't be sliding into it alone.

Not in the six years since Bernard's death would she have described herself as lonely. Yet tonight, she felt that emotion quite keenly.

Oh, hell.

She wished she hadn't dismissed Cecilia's matchmaking efforts so hastily. She did want Dare. For tonight, at least.

Pouting, she altered her direction and went toward the dressing chamber. She stopped short, gasping as a large figure appeared before her.

"Dare!"

"Forgive me for barging in. It was the best way to reach you, I'm afraid."

She took in his banyan, dark black silk against his black pantaloons. "You look like a man on his way to an assignation."

He glanced down at his costume and gave her a fleeting smile. "I suppose I do. But then I am." His gaze met hers. "Hopefully."

Juno hesitated. He was behaving rather presumptuously. But was he really, given her behavior in the coach? She'd certainly given him the impression she wanted him. And anyway, didn't she?

She narrowed her eyes. "How did you find your way here?"

"Luck?" He was clearly lying and realized she knew it. Exhaling, he said, "Lady Cosford told me how."

Juno swore, which drew a broad grin from him. "Why are you smiling?"

"I like it when you curse."

She swallowed a laugh. "It's horribly crude. I shouldn't do it. I'm afraid it was a bad habit of Bernard's, and once I adopted it, I haven't been able to shake it. Unless I'm in polite company, of course." She flinched. "I didn't mean to insinuate you aren't polite company."

He didn't look insulted in the slightest. "No need to feel bad. I'm quite flattered. I hope you'll swear in front of me often." He smiled again, and her heart flipped over.

"You're so handsome when you smile. Irresistible, really. It's good that you rarely do, for every woman in England would throw herself at your feet."

He stepped toward her until they were merely a breath apart. "I don't want every woman in England. Just you." His voice, always tinged with a growl, had dropped to a feral rasp.

If she hadn't wanted him already, she definitely would now. She slid her hands up his chest and curled them around his neck. "It's very convenient, then, that I want you too."

He clasped her in his arms and lifted her against him as their mouths crashed together. If she hadn't been wearing a dressing gown and night rail, she would have wrapped her legs around his hips.

Not that she would have had much time to do so, for he carried her to the bed and pushed her down on the mattress as he came over her. He pulled back, staring down at her. "Wait." He traced his hand across her forehead, along the side of her face, across her lips, and down her chin and throat. He moved lower still, his eyes never leaving hers as he trailed his fingers between her breasts. He unfastened the clasps holding her gown together and spread the garment open.

"You're more beautiful than I imagined." He cupped her breast through the thin lawn of her night rail.

"You can take it off," she whispered, need

pulsing through her along with a deliciously sweet longing.

"I will. Soon." He pinched her nipple, sending a cascade of pleasure straight to her core.

She arched up into his touch, gasping. "More. Please."

He did as she asked, pulling on her flesh with a gentle but firm grasp. Heat flooded her. It wasn't enough, and yet it was perfect.

She pushed up from the bed and struggled to pull her arms from the dressing gown. He helped strip it away, leaving her in just her night rail, which seemed an offensive barrier at the moment.

"Patience, darling," he admonished, pushing her back down.

"I want it off. Touch me, please."

He did, but through the fabric of the night rail. It was both enticing and frustrating. She wriggled beneath him as his mouth descended on her breast, his lips and tongue tormenting first one nipple, then the other. He alternated between sharply tugging on her and gently laving. She panted with need, wondering if she'd ever been this aroused.

"Have I tortured you enough?" he asked huskily, his hand moving to her thigh. He pushed the garment up to her waist.

"More, please." She spread her legs, inviting him to touch her there as he'd done in the coach. But he didn't. Instead, he slid the night rail up her abdomen and over her breasts, moving with a slowness that made every sensation more intense.

He gripped the fabric in his fist, pulling it against her upper arms and across the top of her breasts as he lowered his head and took her nipple into his mouth. Sucking hard, he moved his other hand between her legs, his fingers grazing her sex with light, tantalizing strokes.

She wanted him to claim all of her. She wanted more of what she'd tasted that afternoon. How had she ever thought she could just leave without a night like this?

She ran her fingers through his thick, dark hair as she'd longed to do. "Dare, I need—"

He stroked her clitoris as he drew on her nipple, and she writhed with pleasure. "What do you need?"

"Everything." She pulled at his banyan. "Can we start with you naked, please?"

"You're so polite. Even now," he murmured against her. "Do you ever lose control?"

"What do you mean?"

"I mean, do you forget to say please? Do you ever demand instead of ask? Take instead of invite?"

Her blood heated. "No. Not really."

He straightened, leaving her cold and bereft. She whimpered softly as he removed his banyan. Underneath, he wore a shirt, which she found horribly disappointing. Thankfully, he removed it with great speed, exposing his incredibly muscular chest, covered with dark hair.

Standing between her legs at the edge of the side of the bed, he splayed his palm over her lower abdomen, just above her sex. Her body twitched with need, her breasts aching for him to touch them again.

He narrowed his dark eyes at her. "Put your arms up over your head and clasp your hands together."

She did as he commanded, her breath coming in short pants.

"I love what that does to your breasts." His gaze dipped to her chest in appreciation.

"Touch them. Please."

He shook his head. "No more please. If you use that word, I won't do it."

She arched a brow at him. "You want me to be disagreeable like you?"

He chuckled low in his throat. "I want you to lose control. Leave the charming companion somewhere else. Right now, in this bed, I want Juno. I want the goddess who can't stand it when I don't touch her."

Goddess? She was surprised to realize he made her feel like one. "Touch me. *Now.*"

"What shall I touch you with? My hand?" He wriggled his fingers. "My mouth? Or my cock?"

"All of them. Pl—" She pressed her lips together. "Hands on my breasts—I like when you squeeze my nipples. Mouth on my sex."

His lips curled into the most alluring smile she'd seen on his face yet. She swore she grew even more wet just from that.

He put both hands on her, gently stroking her for a moment. "Happy to oblige." He pinched her nipples, pulling until she cried out in ecstasy. "Like that, then?"

"*Yes.*"

Repeating the motions, he pinched and pulled as he kissed her mouth, his tongue claiming her while she twisted beneath him. She clung to him, her fingers digging into his scalp and shoulders. She wrapped her legs around his waist and arched up against his groin. The length of his cock, still covered by his pantaloons, pressed into her sex, sending a wave of white-light pleasure through her.

"Not yet," he murmured before kissing down her throat. He stopped at her breasts, alternating his mouth and fingers on each until she was on the edge of release. She'd never gotten there like this before. The depth of her desire for him was astonishing.

His lips trailed down her abdomen, moving meticulously as he kept up his attention on one breast. His other hand slipped down between her legs and teased her folds.

"So wet and ready for me. But I think I need to taste you first. The sample I had earlier wasn't nearly enough." His mouth descended on her sex, his thumb pressing on her clitoris as he licked along her flesh.

She gripped his head as he skimmed his hand from her breast to her hip. He brought her leg onto his shoulder and thrust his tongue inside her.

The orgasm that had been lingering just beyond reach rushed toward her. She was both desperate for release and didn't want the anticipation to end. Ultimately, there was no choice. He stroked her clitoris, then sucked her flesh until she cried out, her muscles clenching as she came. She froze for a moment, her body caught in that state of sheer ecstasy when she felt as if she floated somewhere outside herself. Wave after wave crashed over her, and he was relentless, his fingers and mouth working her until she was completely spent.

Her legs began to quiver, and she opened her eyes to see he was removing his pantaloons. His cock sprang free, tall and hard amidst a nest of dark hair.

She licked her lips, and he groaned. "Next time, Juno. Right now, I'm going to slide so deep inside you that we'll have no notion of where one of us ends and the other begins."

His words tantalized her, but it was more than that. They carried weight, a promise of something that went beyond this physical joining.

No, she wouldn't think of that. They had

tonight, this blissful moment, and that would be enough.

"Take me, Dare," she demanded, doing as he told her. Pushing up from the mattress, she rearranged herself lengthwise on the bed and spread her legs in invitation. She reached for his cock, curling her hand around the hard velvet shaft.

His hips jerked and he climbed onto the bed, settling between her thighs. Slipping his hands beneath her backside, he tilted her hips. She bent her legs and guided him to her sex. His flesh nudged at hers, and passion tightened within her once more. She'd thought she was spent, but she had much more to give.

Juno gripped his backside and pulled him into her, squeezing her legs around him. He thrust deep, just as he said he would.

She wanted him hard and fast, her body eager for another release. But he moved slowly, sliding in and out as he kissed her.

"Faster, Dare."

"Shhh. In a moment. This is the greatest moment of my life, and I'm going to enjoy it."

Pleasure flushed through her and she kissed him back with a fervent sweetness, wanting to sear this memory onto her brain for all time.

"You're so beautiful," he whispered, his body moving over and within her. "So joyful. My world was so much darker before you walked into it."

Emotion welled inside her. Then he began to move fast, and she lost herself in the rhythm of their bodies gliding together. Rapture built, and she fell over the edge once more, mindless as he drove into her until his orgasm swept him away.

She felt him tense just before he cried out. It started as that low, wonderful growl and ended with something primal that made her shiver.

Holding him tightly, she kissed him—shoulder, cheek, forehead, mouth. How could she let him go after this?

She wouldn't. Not yet.

"Do you mind if I stay awhile?" he asked softly, his lips grazing hers.

"Not at all. But you have to go before the maid comes to light the fire. It's still dark."

He nodded as he slipped to her side and onto his back. "We won't get caught." He looked over at her. "Will you ride with me in the morning so I can prove to you that it's not overrated?"

She laughed softly, rotating so she faced him. Placing her hand on his chest, she ran her fingertips through the dark hair between his nipples. "I'd planned to leave tomorrow, but you offer a compelling reason to stay. I will ride with you. Thankfully, I have a riding habit. It's quite smart."

One of his brows arched. "You don't ride, but you have a costume for it?"

"I always try to be prepared. And I'm afraid I have a crushing vulnerability for clothing."

"Do you? I noticed you are rather well dressed for a companion."

"I'm not your typical companion," she said coyly.

He smiled, and she knew she would never tire of seeing him do so. "No, you are not. You are exceptional in every way." He turned and pulled her braid over her shoulder. His fingers began to pluck her hair free. When it was loose, he arranged it over her shoulder, so the curls caressed her face "This is better."

"Is it?"

"Yes, but it could be even more improved if you climbed on top of me and let it fall against my chest." He rolled to his back. "If you were so inclined."

"As it happens, I am." She straddled him, feeling his cock stiffen against her sex. "It seems you are too," she murmured.

"Exceptional," he breathed as he pulled her head down and kissed her.

CHAPTER 12

"*Y*ou're doing quite well," Dare said as they slowed their horses to a walk after an exhilarating, though brief, gallop.

She cast him a skeptical glance with a wry smile from beneath the jaunty hat crowning her golden curls. "You're lying, but I won't fault you for it."

"I'm not at all. When we started, you said you wouldn't go faster than a canter."

"I shall credit your persistence far more than my comfort in the saddle." She shifted in her seat.

"You look magnificent." She'd been quite right about her habit—she was stunning from head to boot. "Shall we take a respite? There's a small, somewhat hidden folly up ahead."

"Is there? How charming. Yes, a short rest would be delightful."

Dare led her around a copse of trees to where a dilapidated miniature faux temple stood at the apex of a squat, flat hill. Shrubbery and flowers grew wild around it. Not terribly wild, actually, which made Dare believe it was all part of the effect of creating a "ruin."

He dismounted and spoke softly to the horse, telling him to stay put for a bit. Then he went to help Juno down. She put her hands on his shoulders and moved her knee from the pommel. Clasping her firmly, he gently slid her to the ground.

"All right?" he asked.

"It's been ages since I rode. Over a year, at least. I daresay I will be sore tomorrow."

"I hope it will have been worth it."

"Ask me when we get back to the stables." She cast him a sultry glance, then started up the hill toward the folly. "How did you find this?"

He followed her, enjoying the sway of her backside as she climbed. "Lord Cosford told me about it. I've been riding out every morning. The estate is quite nice."

"You like the outdoors a great deal. Do you ride every day?"

"I do. And walk, usually."

She glanced back at him. "And does your estate have a folly?"

"Three. I'm building a fourth. To me, they're outdoor rooms."

"That sounds rather lovely." She reached the top of the hill and turned to face him. "Have you always liked being outside?"

"Yes. My father encouraged it. He wanted me to know and appreciate the land in a way that some of our class do not. The land defines us, gives us purpose, and makes us whole. We could not survive without it."

"What a beautiful sentiment. I hadn't stopped to think about it in that way."

"What did your parents encourage you to do?" he asked, wondering if he'd ever stop being eager to know more about her.

She wrinkled her nose slightly. "Lady things, I suppose. And reading, but that was mostly my grandfather's doing." Her features softened. "I do miss him terribly, but at least he writes."

"Does he?" Dare was inordinately pleased by this information. He'd hated thinking her entire family acted as if she didn't exist. How could they ignore such a vibrant, wonderful person whom they were fortunate enough to call their kin? "I'm glad for you."

"Have you been inside the folly?" She turned and walked toward the small stone structure. Four pillars stood along the front, and a set of steps led up to the interior. The roof was partially open, as if half of it had collapsed. Inside, there was a bench, and the back wall was solid.

"I have. The bench is an excellent place for contemplation."

She moved inside and sauntered behind the stone seat. "What did you contemplate?"

"Whether Lady Marina and I were compatible. Why the devil I agreed to come to this party. How much I wanted a certain companion."

Facing him, she fixed him with a provocative stare. "How much was that?"

He stalked toward her, lust roaring through him. "Less than I do now, but still a rather staggering amount."

"It's too bad this folly isn't equipped with a bed." She tipped her head back as he stopped in front of her. "Are any of yours?"

Inhaling her scent, he traced his fingertip along her jaw. "Not yet. Anyway, I can make do. That is, if you'd like me to."

"I most definitely would." She slid her hands up his coat as he lowered his head to kiss her.

Fire and delight sparked through him the moment their lips touched. Groaning, he clasped her to him and plundered her mouth. She clung to him, kissing him back with passionate abandon.

He guided her back to the wall, pressing her against it. She gasped, and he pulled back, asking, "What's wrong?"

"The stone is a bit cold. But I don't care." She dug her fingers into him, and he kissed her again.

Driven by need, he cupped her breast, frustrated by the layers of clothing separating them. Using his teeth, he removed his glove, tossing it aside, then clutched at her skirts, wresting them upward.

She took them from him, freeing his hand so he could stroke her. "Yes, please," she rasped. "No, I mean, touch me, Dare. Make me come."

Her words made his cock twitch with want. "How shall I do that?" he asked, sliding his fingertip along her folds as he kissed her neck. "With my hand like this?" He caressed her clitoris, then thrust two fingers into her wet sheath. "Or perhaps with my mouth."

"Your cock." She gripped his head, dislodging his hat so it fell to the ground. "I want your cock. All of it. *Now*."

How he'd found a woman like this at a bloody house party of all places would never cease to astound him. "I will never hate another house party," he muttered as he unbuttoned his fall.

She laughed softly. "I'm so glad to have changed your mind about them." Her hand joined his as he pulled his shaft from his smallclothes. She stroked him, and he savored her touch for a moment, his eyes closing and his head falling back. She'd taken him in her mouth last night, rather, early this morning before he'd left her bed. The memory nearly made him orgasm in her hand.

"Enough." He gripped her hips. "Put your legs around me."

He lifted her, pressing her against the wall as she curled her thighs around his hips. She tucked her hand between them and guided his shaft inside her. He thrust deep, holding her steady against the stone as he seated himself within her.

She moaned—loudly, which only fanned his desire—and clenched her legs around him. It was all the urging he needed.

"Hold on to me," he ordered, rubbing against her before he began to move. He drove hard and fast, careful not to hurt her.

"Yes, Dare. Just like that." She kissed his cheek, his jaw, then gently bit his earlobe. *"Faster."*

She *was* a goddess, and he would worship at her altar for the rest of his days. He pounded into her, feeling her muscles clench around him as she clamored for release.

Then she came in a torrent of cries and desperation, her fingers digging into his neck and shoulder. He cast his head back, his balls tightening, and cried out as rapture claimed him.

When his body unfurled, he slowly lowered her to the ground, but he didn't let go. He guided her to the bench, sitting her down so she could collect herself.

He leaned back against the wall and closed his eyes, panting as he fought to regain his breath. Perhaps he ought to build a fifth folly. With a bed.

Grinning, he opened his eyes to find her watching him. "I think I've proved without question that riding is not overrated."

Juno tipped her head to the side, then slowly rose from the bench. "I think the opposite is true. When you think of this ride, what will you remember most? I daresay it won't be the actual riding." She gave him a saucy smile.

He shouted with laughter and grabbed her to him. "I am corrected, my goddess. I have never been more happy to be wrong."

Actually, he'd just never been more happy.

~

*I*f the riding didn't make Juno sore, all the sexual intercourse she and Dare had engaged in over the past twenty-four hours would. She didn't think she'd ever spent so much time in bed not sleeping. Not that all their activities had occurred in bed. She would remember their tryst in the folly to the end of her days.

She'd been loath to get back on the horse after that, but she'd managed. They'd ridden straight back to the stables, and then she'd stayed away from him the rest of the day. Avoiding him lest they spark any rumors, she'd spent the afternoon with Lady Gilpin, who'd told her all about Presley, their estate where Juno would come to live and work with Dorothy.

Typically, Juno would be filled with an excited anticipation. However, she found herself feeling sad about leaving Dare. She was only disappointed because she was used to her liaisons lasting longer than a few days. This time with Dare would be abbreviated—the party was only two more days—which was a pity since he was the finest lover she'd ever known.

She looked over at him, dozing next to her in the bed. He'd stolen in through the dressing chamber as he'd done the night before. They hadn't discussed it, but they'd known it would happen. All during dinner—where they'd sat next to each other again thanks to their matchmaking hostess—there'd been an undercurrent of desire swirling between them. She'd barely kept herself from touching him. In fact, she'd managed to stroke his thigh a few times during the meal. He'd done the same with her.

There was no sweeter torture or richer anticipation than a secret affair.

She turned and snuggled back against his side, closing her eyes. Tomorrow, they were going to play chess. And perhaps find a cupboard to shag in.

"Mmm." He growled against her nape, his arm coming around her and cupping her breast. He pinched her nipple, drawing a low moan from her throat.

"Shouldn't we sleep?" she asked, even as desire pulsed between her legs.

"Wasn't I just sleeping?" He played with her breast as his cock hardened against her backside.

"I wasn't." She sighed as he trailed his hand down her abdomen. He stroked her clitoris, tracing languorous strokes along her flesh as he teased her arousal into a flame of need.

"Should I let you?" He kissed along her neck and shoulder, nipping her flesh.

"Not *now*." She lifted her knee forward on the mattress, exposing her sex to him in invitation.

"I see. What if I insisted?" He caressed her hip and then her backside, his fingertips sliding down her cleft.

She pressed back, seeking his touch, needing him inside her. "You're being a terrible tease."

"Yes." He stroked her flesh, everywhere but the place she wanted him.

"Are you going to put yourself inside me or not?" Frustration began to war with her desire.

"Like this?" He speared his fingers into her.

"Oh, yes." She closed her eyes and moved with him, her hip sliding along the bedclothes as he coaxed her to completion.

Then he was gone, but only for a moment. He guided his cock into her and took her on a slow, languid journey. They moved together, his hand caressing her breast, hers stroking his thigh. This was a level of bliss she'd never experienced. Just when she wasn't sure how much more she could take, he rotated, pressing her down into the mattress as his hips snapped against her backside.

Squeezing her nipple, he ordered her to come. Unable to deny him, she fell apart, her body stiffening as an enormous wave of ecstasy swept over her.

He gripped her tightly and spent himself inside her. Kissing her shoulder, he gently eased from her.

Juno smiled, feeling so utterly satisfied and wonderful. "Come to Bath with me when the party is over."

"I can't."

She rolled over to face him. "Why not?"

"I have to be in London to supervise renovations at my house."

"Really?" She pushed her hair behind her ear. "Surely you can delay that and come to spend a few days with me before I go to Presley."

"I can't. My plans have been set for weeks."

She leaned up on her elbow and put her head on her hand. "It's only a few days. Just a small change to your plans. Hardly significant."

He frowned. "Of course it is. I'm expected in London."

Oh dear, the rigid duke had returned.

"I understand it can be difficult for you to alter your plans, but I know you can do it." She gave him an encouraging smile.

"No, I cannot." He sat up, his features set into a surly glower she hadn't seen all day. "Perhaps you should come to London with me instead."

"I can't do that. I need to return home before I go to Presley. A trip to London wouldn't allow that."

"Then perhaps you shouldn't be going to Presley."

Juno sat up, holding the coverlet to her chest. "I should come to London with you, trailing after you like a mistress?" She'd never allowed others' expectations to dictate her choices—her marriage to Bernard and the subsequent loss of her family being the prime example. That Dare would ask such a thing of her cut to the quick. "I am an independent woman, Dare. I don't trail after anyone. I make my own choices. For *me*. Perhaps you should go." Emotion made her quiver. She squeezed the coverlet tightly to try to make it stop.

He slid from the bed. "I will." He snatched up his banyan and tugged it on. Scowling, he grabbed his shirt and pantaloons from the end of the bed and thrust his feet into his slippers—at least it seemed that was what he was doing since she couldn't see over the edge of the bed.

Half turning, he sent her a frown. "You can't expect me to change my plans. Or who I am. I thought you knew me."

"I do," she said quietly, exhaling. She thought she did anyway, but what did it matter? It seemed he didn't really know her. But what had she expected? This had been a lovely interlude. One they'd known would end.

Still, his expectation that she change her plans and conform to his reminded her too much of her parents and their painful abandonment. She'd forgotten the depth of his rigidity, and it was good

that he'd reminded her. He'd saved her future disappointment.

Dare left without another word. She stared at
the emptiness and felt it deep in her bones.

Yes, it was time for this to end. She needed to
get back to her life.

CHAPTER 13

*D*are had barely slept the night before last and had still felt positively wonderful the following day. He'd actually gotten a little more sleep last night and yet today felt like he'd been dragged behind a coach. Sleep, it seemed, had nothing to do with anything. Happiness—or a lack thereof—did.

There was no happiness today, just misery. He'd taken a brutally long ride that morning and had spent the last hour, or perhaps two, walking. Anything to avoid the house.

No, to avoid Juno.

Except he wasn't really avoiding her. Not completely, anyway. He'd spent time at their folly—it would forevermore be *their* folly—and was now lingering outside the orangery.

Why was he being so...rigid? Because he didn't know how not to be. He was expected in London. He *needed* to go to London. He certainly couldn't upend his life to continue a liaison with a young lady's companion.

Why not?

He growled, his lip curling. Because spending a few days with her in Bath before she left him to go to her next job was unacceptable. It was too short a time. That she'd expected it of him made him think she hadn't really come to know him at all.

Sorrow ate at his insides. He thought she *had* come to understand him, in spite of his quirks and general disagreeability. For the first time in his life, he'd made a connection with someone that seemed mutually beneficial. She absolutely made him a better man—he was certain of that. And he'd rather thought he'd had a positive influence on her, and it had nothing to do with his status.

Perhaps he was wrong about that. She'd had no hesitation in simply going on with her life, pursuing her work without sparing a thought for him. It seemed she hadn't been as affected by him as he was by her. The notion was a knife twisting in his chest. He'd thought he'd found someone who finally saw past his outer shell, who made him feel comfortable—and accepted—at last.

This pain pricking through him was the reason he'd left last night. He hadn't been able to see past what felt like her abandonment of him and what they'd found together.

Except she invited you to Bath. Clearly, she wasn't abandoning you, not completely. Furthermore, going with her would have given you more time with her, and isn't that what you want?

It was. He didn't want the happiness he'd unexpectedly and miraculously found with her to end. And yet he'd behaved like an ass, insisting he couldn't alter his precious plans, proving to her that he was inflexible and demanding—*rigid*. He suddenly thought of her family and their inflexibility—and rigidity—when she'd married and they hadn't approved. His behavior wasn't much better. But that was who he was, wasn't it?

No. He wanted to change everything for her.

She deserved the best he could give her. She'd certainly evoked that in him. She'd given him joy, anticipation, love.

Love?

The word hit him like a stone. Could he love her? He'd felt strong passion, but never love. It was a messy, unnecessary emotion. Except right now, it felt as critical to him as breathing.

He loved her. Desperately. The thought of only sharing a few days with her made him feel ill. But the thought of never spending time with her again made him feel much, much worse.

The urge to go to the house and tell her was overwhelming, but he hesitated. What if she didn't feel the same? She was a strong, independent woman, eager to get on with her plans—which didn't include him. She didn't need him.

But was there a chance she wanted him? Would she be willing to give up the life she'd created for herself to become his duchess? That was quite a shift—for both of them. It was absolutely what he wanted. He knew that with a soul-deep certainty.

Dare paced behind the orangery, his stride changing speed as new thoughts arrested his brain. None of this had been in his plans. It was no wonder he was in a dither. He stopped, forcing himself to take a deep breath.

He loved her. He'd behaved like an ass last night, and if he let her go without telling her both those things, he'd regret it to the end of his days. And he'd already decided he wasn't going to suffer regret.

Pivoting, he stalked to the house and went in search of his goddess. Would she be in her room? He heard voices from the drawing room and went there instead. It was a good place to start.

"Here is the duke!" Lady Cosford said warmly

as he paused just inside the threshold. She was perched on a settee and was speaking with Lady Bentham and Mrs. Hadley. Both ladies perused him, and he realized he was still in his outdoor clothing. He probably should have gone to change.

He scanned the room in search of Juno. Most of the guests were present. But not her. Damn.

Moving another few steps into the room, he fixed his attention on Lady Cosford. "Might I speak with you a moment?" he asked quietly but loud enough for her to hear.

"Of course." She rose from the settee and joined him. Then they moved back toward the doorway.

Dare got right to the point. "I wonder if you could tell me where I might find Mrs. Langton?"

Lady Cosford's brow furrowed. "I'm sorry, but she's gone."

The world seemed to fade around Dare. His lungs squeezed and his appendages felt odd, as if they weren't even there. She was gone. It was over.

No, it's not, you idiot. Go after her.

He twitched, rolling his shoulders. "Where did she go?"

"She went to Bath."

"When?"

"An hour ago?" Lady Cosford looked uncertain.

"How can you not know?" His voice began to rise as all the wonderful emotions he'd just fucking recognized begin to melt away.

None of this was supposed to happen. He wasn't supposed to have fallen in love or have been stupid enough to let her go.

"We can ask the stable when she left. She took one of our coaches." Lady Cosford spoke in a calm, helpful manner, but it did nothing to alleviate his agitation.

"Is there something amiss?" Lady Bentham

called from somewhere. Dare had tunnel vision at the moment and could only see his hostess. Truthfully, he couldn't even really see her. He saw Juno, but she was so terribly far away. Could he ever get to her? Was he too late?

Dare's heart pounded a harsh, staccato rhythm. Cold sweat dappled the back of his neck.

"Are you all right?" Lady Cosford asked, sounding as if she were down a hole.

"He doesn't look all right." Lady Bentham again, closer than before, but still as if she were behind something.

He felt a touch on his arm and instantly jerked away, stepping to the side. He blinked, and the room came into focus. What the hell had just happened to him?

Looking about wildly, he found Lady Cosford. "I need to go after her. Immediately." He wasn't even going to change clothes.

"I'll have your coach prepared," Lady Cosford said.

"What a magnificent surprise this is," Lady Bentham murmured. "And how titillated the ton will be."

Lady Cosford turned on the older woman, her eyes narrowed. "Have you no shame?"

"I have plenty, but not about this," she said with a laugh. She looked to Dare. "The duke knows how the world works. He knew the minute he declared his intent to pursue Mrs. Langton that his secret—whatever the specifics are—is out in the world. To think those present in this room wouldn't share such delightful information is beneath his intelligence."

She was right. But he hadn't considered it before he'd spoken. He hadn't thought about it at all. There had been no strategy to his utterance, just a primal need to reach the woman he loved. Juno would be thrilled that his rigidity had been nowhere in sight.

Buoyed by this, he turned to Lady Bentham. "It's not a secret. I am in love with Mrs. Langton and need to tell her so as soon as possible. If it makes you happy to spread that information, then by all means do so. Honestly, I don't care if the entire world knows. Although, I would prefer she heard it from me," he said wryly, surprised and grateful that his equilibrium had mostly returned.

"I just did."

Dare thought he was hearing things. But he turned to the doorway and she was there. His goddess had returned.

~

*J*uno stared at Dare, thinking she couldn't have heard him right. He loved her? And he'd said so in front of everyone in this room?

Every guest present was focused intently on the drama playing out just inside the threshold. Juno wondered what she'd missed. Although, she wasn't sure it mattered. Not if he'd actually said what she thought she'd heard.

"You came back," Dare said simply, his features radiating joy. It was an odd thing to behold, and Juno had to blink, as if she were looking at the sun.

"I did," she said slowly. "Did I just hear—"

"Me say that I love you. Yes. I was an ass. An inflexible, overthinking, single-minded curmudgeon. Who would like to beg your forgiveness."

"Are you sure you want to have this conversation here?" she whispered, glancing particularly at

Lady Bentham, who was watching—and listening to—them with rapt interest.

"I do. I don't care who hears what I have to say." His brow creased. "Unless you do. Perhaps you'd prefer I close my mouth and never speak again."

She couldn't help smiling, overcome with joy that he would put her feelings in front of his. She'd been so wrong to compare him to her parents, to forget that he struggled with his inflexibility. "I admit I'm shocked to hear you say so much, let alone display…so much, but I am quite delighted to hear whatever you have to say however you wish to say it." If she cared about her professional future as a companion, she would silence him. However, she was fairly certain her role as a companion was already at risk since Lady Gilpin was seated nearby, and her attention was completely focused on them.

Furthermore, she could see Dare's rigid outer shell cracking apart, and she couldn't bring herself to stop that. This was an important moment for him. And hopefully for them together.

He dropped to his knee before her, and several gasps filled the air. Juno's heart picked up speed, clamoring against her ribs as happiness and anticipation collided in her chest.

"In addition to begging your forgiveness—"

"You have it," she cut in, not wanting him to go another moment thinking she was angry or disappointed. "There's nothing to forgive. I should have been more understanding. I do know you, and I love all your eccentricities."

His lips curved into the most dazzling smile he'd yet displayed. Juno had to keep herself from leaping onto him and tackling him to the carpet.

"You love me?"

She nodded.

"How unexpected," he murmured, taking her hand. "And wonderful. In addition to begging forgiveness, when apparently none is required, I also planned to use this opportunity to beg you to be my wife. Juno, my goddess, will you do me the honor of becoming my duchess?"

A duchess! Juno had considered many options when she'd decided to turn the coach around and return to Blickton, including marriage. However, she'd instantly determined that would never happen. What duke would propose to a paid companion? Particularly a duke with rigid plans and expectations.

She clapped her free hand over her mouth as emotion overwhelmed her. She hadn't expected him to say he loved her. And she'd certainly never imagined *this*.

"You planned?" was all she could manage to say, briefly lowering her hand to her chin.

He arched one of his gloriously thick brows at her. "You can't be surprised by that?"

A giggle slipped from her mouth, and she moved her hand back up to seal her lips. Inhaling through her nose, she dropped her hand and tried to calm the torrent inside her. "No, I should not be surprised."

"Are you going to give him an answer?" Lady Bentham demanded, grinning.

"Yes," Juno said softly, reaching to caress Dare's cheek. "Yes, I will marry you, though I can't imagine why you would choose me."

He frowned at her, looking much more like the rigid duke, whom she also loved. "Because you're intelligent, witty, strong, charming, and you make me smile."

"That last part should be enough," Lady Bentham said drolly. "You may be the only person in existence who can do that."

A small smile broke across Dare's lips, and Juno laughed. "Not true, Lady Bentham. But your point is well taken." She squeezed his hand. "I will spend the rest of my life making you smile so much that your lips will want to fall off."

He stood and lifted her hand to press a kiss to her wrist. "I shall pray that does *not* happen, because my lips are of particular and essential use to me. And to you," he added in a husky whisper.

"You make a better point than Lady Bentham," she said softly, her chest tight from an overwhelming barrage of emotion. She'd never felt this full, not even when she'd fallen for Bernard. That had been a different sensation, she realized, a young love rife with enthusiasm and passion. This was mature and whole, and loving him made her feel…right. Which was something, since she hadn't felt at all wrong. Indeed, she'd been perfectly content with her life. So content that she'd almost talked herself out of coming back. Until she'd finally acknowledged that Dare had quite destroyed that contentment when he'd glowered his way into her life. It seemed that love came when one least expected it.

"I have to tell you," she whispered up at Dare. "This isn't what I expected. I thought we would form an attachment, but not marriage. I made a commitment to Lady Gilpin, and I don't feel right abandoning her." She glanced toward her almost employer with a pang of guilt.

"Of course you don't," he said. "You're as loyal as the day is long. Do you still want to help her?"

"I do. But—and I want to be very clear on this point—my primary loyalty is to you. To us."

"You humble me." His voice was deep and soft,

his expression full of love. He slipped his arm around her waist and pivoted them toward Lady Gilpin. "If it's acceptable to you, Mrs. Langton will still help your daughter prepare for the Season. After we are wed."

Lady Gilpin's eyes rounded. She lifted her hand to her chest. "That, ah, that isn't necessary."

"Perhaps not, but Juno's word is her bond, and she would very much like to honor her commitment."

"It would give me great pleasure to help Dorothy for my final act as a companion," Juno added, loving Dare so much for his support.

"Then yes," Lady Gilpin said with a grateful smile. "We would be thrilled to have the Duchess of Warrington prepare our daughter for her Season."

Put like that, Dorothy was bound to have an unforgettable debut. Juno would make sure of it.

"Well, I think this calls for a celebratory dinner," Cecilia said, beaming. She gave Juno a look of pure delight and gently inclined her head.

Thank you, Juno mouthed.

"Can we leave now?" Dare murmured against her ear.

"Yes." She looked about the room. "See you at dinner."

Then she and Dare left the drawing room, and he steered her outside.

"The orangery?" she asked.

"Seems fitting." He held the door open for her as she stepped inside the warm building.

Moving farther inside, she sensed he wasn't behind her. Turning, she saw him standing against the closed door, his gaze fixed on her with dark intent.

She shivered, but in the best way. "I really am sorry for not being more understanding last night.

I shouldn't have been so demanding. In hindsight, I was afraid that you were abandoning me as my parents did."

He rushed toward her and took her in his arms. "My dearest, I could never do that. It will be torture for me when you go to help Lady Gilpin's daughter."

She kissed him, joy threatening to swallow her whole. "It will be torture for me as well."

"As to you being demanding, what did I tell you about that?" he growled, kindling her desire. "I want you to do that with me. Always. One of the things I love most about you is your complete impatience for my nonsense. You make me a better man."

"That was never my intent." She caressed his cheek. "I'd never met anyone so stoic. You provoked me to provoke you. I never meant to change you, and I shouldn't have expected you to do that last night."

"I like that I'm less rigid—with you, at least. I don't give a damn what anyone else thinks." He kissed her again. "Only what you think."

"I think I'm glad that we both realized we're better together than apart." She bit her lip. "I just hope people—such as your family—are accepting of me."

"My mother will adore you because I do. In fact, I can't wait for you to meet her. I'm more concerned about your family."

"Why? They don't even signify."

"I think they do," he said softly. "I intend to drag them back into your life, and if you decide you don't want them there, then it is us who will do the ignoring. Not them."

Emotion clogged her throat. "You are the very best man. My mother will be shocked I am marrying a duke." She shook her head. "I'm not sure I'll believe it until it's true."

"I thought we'd wed by special license since you have other obligations. Is that acceptable to you?"

She met his eyes with love and gratitude. "It's more than acceptable. It's lovely. Where do you want to have the ceremony?"

"London—and not because I *need* to go there." He rolled his eyes, making her laugh. "That will be easiest for obtaining the license. I'll send for my mother to meet us there, if that's all right with you."

"That would be splendid."

"I'll write to your father informing him of my intent. Shall I invite them to come too? I expect we'll be married within the week, so if they can't make it in time, that's too bad."

She stood on her toes and kissed him. "I love you so, my rigid duke."

He wrapped his arms around her, pulling her close. "I'm trying not to be. Rigid, that is."

Rotating her hips against his to press against his hard cock, she said, "I would say you're failing quite spectacularly. And I have no complaints about that. In fact, promise me you'll never stop."

He threw his head back and laughed with abandon, something a rigid duke would never do. "You have my sincerest vow, my goddess." He lowered his mouth to hers and kissed her thoroughly. Then he drew back and looked into her eyes. "My love for you is firm and unchangeable. Forever."

EPILOGUE

London

"Checkmate."

Dare stared at the board. He'd seen it coming, of course, but he was still astounded at how far her skill had come in such a short time. He should not have been, however, since she was the cleverest woman he'd ever known. "Well done," he murmured with great admiration, his gaze finding hers.

She grinned with pride and looked toward his mother, who sat nearby doing needlework. "I won, Mama." The dowager had insisted her new daughter-in-law call her Mama. She adored Juno, just as Dare had predicted.

"Huzzah!" His mother put down her needlework and reached for her glass of sherry. "A toast to the duchess and her victory!"

Dare picked up his glass of port at the same moment Juno did the same. They all lifted their glasses and took a drink.

"It's too bad your parents and grandfather left

this morning," his mother went on. "I daresay the baron would have been thrilled with your triumph."

The baron had been surprisingly charming. Dare had liked him a great deal. Her parents were less...likeable, but that was probably because Dare was holding a grudge for the way they'd treated Juno these past several years. He hadn't been able to resist pointing out that their daughter had married without their permission yet again, though it seemed this one was more to their taste. Juno had elbowed him sharply for that. Then later, she'd tended his (nonexistent) hurt and thanked him gleefully for being the best husband ever.

"I think I'll turn in." Dare's mother stood and bid them good night. "I shall miss you when you're off with your charge," she said to Juno.

"I'll miss you too, Mama," Juno said warmly. "But we'll be together again for Yuletide, and then you'll come back to London for the Season."

"I can hardly wait. Good night, my lovelies." She gave Dare the same look she'd bestowed on him since she'd arrived in London to meet Juno—one of absolute love and gratitude. She was so very happy that he was happy.

And that made him even happier. He'd turned into soft pulp or whatever was the opposite of rigid.

"Hmm, should we go up to bed too?" Juno asked. "We've only two more nights until I leave for Presley."

"I'm beginning to think I should come with you."

She shook her head. "No, you'd be a huge distraction, and I can't have that. Even though I didn't really fail with Marina, I still feel the need for this to be my most successful position yet."

"Of course you didn't fail with her," he said softly. "She has told you as much." Lady Marina had written to them upon hearing of their betrothal and wished them every happiness. She'd seemed in good spirits—at least on paper.

"I suppose not. I do hope I'll get to see her in the new year at some point. Perhaps during the Season. In the meantime, our separation is only a month."

"Closer to five weeks," he corrected.

"I love that you are aware of every day we'll be apart. The time will fly, and then I'll be with you for the holidays." She stood from her chair and came around the small table.

He pushed his chair back, angling it so he could pull her onto his lap. "I'm still coming to fetch you. I insist. In fact, I should also deliver you. That would give us two more days—and one night together." He buried his face in her neck and kissed her warm flesh.

"Two nights, actually, since you'd have to stay over at Presley before leaving."

"You're not saying no." His blood heated in anticipation, both for the journey to Presley and for the next ten minutes.

"I suppose I'm not." She ran her hands through his hair, her fingers massaging his scalp as he feasted on her neck and collarbone. "Yes, come with me. But not to stay."

He cupped her nape and pulled her down for a long, torrid kiss. "We'll see if I can't change your mind."

"If anyone can do that, it's you, my love. But then unlike you, I have always been rather flexible."

"Mmm." He kissed her again. "Show me."

Don't miss what happens at the Blickton House Party in 1803, where matchmaking shenanigans and true love abounds! Follow the Matchmaking Chronicles with *The Bachelor Earl* and then continue with *The Runaway Viscount*!

Would you like to know when my next book is available and to hear about sales and deals? Sign up for my VIP newsletter, follow me on social media:

Facebook: https://facebook.com/DarcyBurkeFans
Twitter at @darcyburke
Instagram at darcyburkeauthor
Pinterest at darcyburkewrite

And follow me on Bookbub to receive updates on pre-orders, new releases, and deals!

Need more Regency romance? Check out my other historical series:

The Phoenix Club
Society's most exclusive invitation...

Welcome to the Phoenix Club, where London's most audacious, disreputable, and intriguing ladies and gentlemen find scandal, redemption, and second chances.

The Untouchables
Swoon over twelve of Society's most eligible and elusive bachelor peers and the bluestockings, wallflowers, and outcasts who bring them to their knees!

The Untouchables: The Spitfire Society
Meet the smart, independent women who've decided they don't need Society's rules, their families' expectations, or, most importantly, a husband. But just because they don't need a man doesn't mean they might not *want* one...

The Untouchables: The Pretenders
Set in the captivating world of The Untouchables, follow the saga of a trio of siblings who excel at being something they're not. Can a dauntless Bow Street Runner, a devastated viscount, and a disillusioned Society miss unravel their secrets?

Wicked Dukes Club
Six books written by me and my BFF, NYT Bestselling Author Erica Ridley. Meet the unforgettable men of London's most notorious tavern, The Wicked Duke. Seductively handsome, with charm and wit to spare, one night with these rakes and rogues will never be enough...

Love is All Around
Heartwarming Regency-set retellings of classic Christmas stories (written after the Regency!) featuring a cozy village, three siblings, and the best gift of all: love.

Secrets and Scandals
Six epic stories set in London's glittering ballrooms and England's lush countryside.

Legendary Rogues
Five intrepid heroines and adventurous heroes embark on exciting quests across the Georgian Highlands and Regency England and Wales!

If you like contemporary romance, I hope you'll check out my **Ribbon Ridge** series available from Avon Impulse, and the continuation of Ribbon Ridge in **So Hot**.

I hope you'll consider leaving a review at your favorite online vendor or networking site!

I appreciate my readers so much. Thank you, thank you, *thank you*.

ALSO BY DARCY BURKE

Historical Romance

The Phoenix Club

Invitation (prequel available only to newsletter subscribers)

Improper

Impassioned

Intolerable

Indecent

Impossible

Irresistible

Impeccable

Insatiable

Matchmaking Chronicles

The Rigid Duke

The Bachelor Earl (prequel to The Untouchables)

The Runaway Viscount

The Counterfeit Widow

The Untouchables: The Pretenders

A Secret Surrender

A Scandalous Bargain

A Rogue to Ruin

The Untouchables

The Bachelor Earl (prequel)

The Forbidden Duke

The Duke of Daring

The Duke of Deception

The Duke of Desire

The Duke of Defiance

The Duke of Danger

The Duke of Ice

The Duke of Ruin

The Duke of Lies

The Duke of Seduction

The Duke of Kisses

The Duke of Distraction

The Untouchables: The Spitfire Society

Never Have I Ever with a Duke

A Duke is Never Enough

A Duke Will Never Do

Love is All Around

(A Regency Holiday Trilogy)

The Red Hot Earl

The Gift of the Marquess

Joy to the Duke

Wicked Dukes Club

One Night for Seduction by Erica Ridley

One Night of Surrender by Darcy Burke

One Night of Passion by Erica Ridley

One Night of Scandal by Darcy Burke

One Night to Remember by Erica Ridley

One Night of Temptation by Darcy Burke

Secrets and Scandals

Her Wicked Ways

His Wicked Heart

To Seduce a Scoundrel

To Love a Thief (a novella)

Never Love a Scoundrel

Scoundrel Ever After

Legendary Rogues

The Legend of a Rogue (prequel available only to
newsletter subscribers)

Lady of Desire

Romancing the Earl

Lord of Fortune

Captivating the Scoundrel

Contemporary Romance

Ribbon Ridge

Where the Heart Is (a prequel novella)

Only in My Dreams

Yours to Hold

When Love Happens

The Idea of You

When We Kiss

You're Still the One

Ribbon Ridge: So Hot

So Good

So Right

So Wrong

Prefer to read in German, French, or Italian? Check out
my website for foreign language editions!

ABOUT THE AUTHOR

Darcy Burke is the USA Today Bestselling Author of sexy, emotional historical and contemporary romance. Darcy wrote her first book at age 11, a happily ever after about a swan addicted to magic and the female swan who loved him, with exceedingly poor illustrations. Join her Reader Club newsletter for the latest updates from Darcy.

A native Oregonian, Darcy lives on the edge of wine country with her guitar-strumming husband, artist daughter, and imaginative son who will almost certainly out-write her one day (that may be tomorrow). They're a crazy cat family with two Bengal cats, a small, fame-seeking cat named after a fruit, an older rescue Maine Coon with attitude to spare, an adorable former stray who wandered onto their deck and into their hearts, and two bonded boys who used to belong to (separate) neighbors but chose them instead. You can find Darcy at a winery, in her comfy writing chair balancing her laptop and a cat or three, folding laundry (which she loves), or binge-watching TV with the family. Her happy places are Disneyland, Labor Day weekend at the Gorge, Denmark, and anywhere in the UK—so long as her family is there too. Visit Darcy online at www.darcyburke.com and follow her on social media.

facebook.com/DarcyBurkeFans

twitter.com/darcyburke

instagram.com/darcyburkeauthor

pinterest.com/darcyburkewrites

goodreads.com/darcyburke

bookbub.com/authors/darcy-burke

amazon.com/author/darcyburke